ON THE HUNT

DUOLOGY: INCLUDES BAD BUNNY & JACK RABBIT

SARA LEA

Porkchop Publishing LLC
2709 N Hayden Island Drive STE 417603
Portland, OR 97217

BAD BUNNY

SARA LEA

CHAPTER ONE

BUNNY LIKED BEGINNINGS.

The first brush of powder over skin, the faint chemical sweetness of latex warming in her hands — the calm before anyone spoke her name. In the hush, she could almost believe in herself as a blank surface, something that could be painted into meaning.

She lined up her tools on the counter like surgical instruments: lipstick, wipes, perfume, disinfectant, a coil of pale rope she didn't remember buying. Her apartment was small but orderly, lit by the bluish tremor of a dying fluorescent bulb. Costumes hung on a rack by color and type — a taxonomy of fantasy. Nurse. Nun. Mouse. Fox. Cat. Bear. Predator. Prey.

Behind them, at the far end, hung the rabbit head.

At first, it was not meant to be frightening. The eyes were black glass, perfectly reflective. She'd worn it once for a joke, and a client had gasped — not in fear, but in fascination. Since then, it had become iconic. The rabbit woman. The mask that never blinked.

Her phone buzzed.

CLIENT: Can you wear the rabbit head again?

She smiled, but it wasn't a pleasant expression. Something in her stomach turned over, a slow, hot coil. The request should have been routine. They were all routine. But lately, that head had begun to feel heavier each time she put it on, as if it remembered more than she did.

Bunny moved through her preparations with ritual precision. Shower. Lotion. Hair braided, then hidden. The mirror fogged slightly from her breath. She traced the reflection of her own mouth on the glass, a pale smudge where her lipstick would go.

She thought of her mother's voice, a distant memory: *Smile, sweetheart. Men like you better when you look like you're enjoying it.*

Bunny smiled automatically.

When she reached for the rabbit head, she hesitated. Her hand hovered just above the ear — one of them slightly bent from storage. It stared back at her with those blind eyes, blank and infinite.

A pulse began in her ears, rhythmic and insistent. She slipped the mask on. The world shrank to breath and heartbeat.

Inside, the air smelled faintly of glue and perfume — and something older, something animal.

For a moment, she forgot what her own face looked like.

Later, she stood before the mirror again, fully dressed for the session. The rabbit stared back. Behind the mask, she couldn't see her own eyes, only as movement — twin shadows, restless in their sockets.

"This one's easy," she murmured. "Discipline and forgiveness. He wants to be good."

But the voice that answered in her head wasn't hers.

No one really does.

She turned away quickly, heart stuttering. A trick of nerves, she told herself. Just adrenaline.

Still, when she texted *On my way* and slipped her gloves into her purse, she added something new to the end of her usual checklist — an unspoken promise that had formed somewhere beneath language.

Not just to perform.

To see. To know. To decide.

As she locked the door behind her, her reflection in the hallway mirror lingered a second longer than she did — a pale woman with a rabbit's head, caught mid-turn, as if the mask itself were watching her go.

CHAPTER TWO

SHE MET her client in the hotel room he'd reserved. He'd left the door just open enough that it hadn't latched. She had told him to strip down to his socks and wait for her.

Although she'd been seeing this trick for over a year, she'd come to learn some things about him. She'd originally thought he was a decent man with a proclivity for unusual sexual fetishes. He was well-spoken, and a well-known philanthropist around the city. But through some of their casual conversations, she'd found out he'd misused some funds. Funds meant for charities. And it was even worse.

She was tired of these men taking and taking and taking. Just doing whatever they wanted. They threw money around as if nothing else mattered. As long as they paid to play, they felt entitled for it to be any game of their choosing.

The door clicked closed behind her, locking them in. He whipped his head around and practically panted like a cartoon wolf when he saw her.

"There's my bad little bunny," he said, licking his lips. His excitement became evident. It was all for the rabbit head, because she was still fully clothed.

She knew the drill, so she slipped her dress off, leaving on the stilettos. She was left standing in a crotchless hot pink panties, fishnet stockings, and hot pink bunny head nipple pasties. She did a turn in front of him to reveal the bunny tail glued just above the crack of her ass.

Bending over, she gave him a full view, keeping a hand on the bunny mask so it didn't slide off. She swayed from one side to the other, rotating her hips.

"Hop, bad bunny, hop," he instructed. She did as she was told. His breathing hitched. He liked to watch her and stroke himself first. Every time.

The one thing about the good old charity man was that he was predictable. The same act every time. No surprises. By the time she walked over to him and slid a condom on, he was already almost finished. He put his hands on her hips, thrusting in a few times and then flopped backward, spent.

Mr. Charity Man liked to lie in bed and talk afterwards. It was the part that Bunny usually didn't mind with clients but was coming to loathe as they unloaded their secrets and dirty deeds. Some of them seemed to think that because of the line of work she was in, she was understanding and open to hearing all of their… indiscretions.

Illegal, immoral, unethical… and sometimes downright disturbing. Her regulars seemed to be using her as some kind of confessional booth. Unload and then… unload.

She hadn't really come here tonight with a plan. Or had she? She always kept her small switchblade on her — just in case a trick got out of hand. But tonight she'd lingered on it. Almost like she knew she'd use it, eventually.

As they lay in bed after, he started going on one of his tangents — almost laughing about the funds he'd mishandled. About the funds that had been allocated to an organization that supposedly *helped* children.

Her stomach soured as she listened to the way he talked about it. He never flat-out said the exact words. But she'd been in this city long enough. She knew the organization was a cover for child sex trafficking. And good old Mr. Charity Man — walking around galas, professing his support for these fundraisers — was a regular client of theirs.

He'd made it sound like he was a *good* person when he told Bunny he didn't like it when the kids cried. And that's why he sought out her services. He had a taste for the pure — for the innocent. It's why he had a thing for her as a little white bunny.

"Close your eyes," she whispered in his ear when he paused between stories. Bile burned at the back of her throat. Listening this long had been so hard, but she needed him at his most open — his most vulnerable and trusting self. And here he was, hands propped behind his head.

"Oh, is my little bunny feeling frisky again?" he asked, smiling and tucking his chin to his chest gleefully. He squeezed his eyes shut tight. "I'm ready, little bunny. Hop hop hop."

"Shhh, keep your eyes closed, okay?" she said, slipping a new condom on, and swinging a leg over him to straddle him. She reached for her blade, tucked into a small hidden flap on the side of the mask. She pulled the slim blade out, not taking her eyes off his face.

Placing a hand on his chest, she leaned her weight down on him. He shifted, and just as he opened his eyes, she swiped her blade clean across his throat. She pulled back as the blood spurted out, trying to avoid getting it on her mask.

He blinked in confusion, his body bucking against her, choking and coughing out blood. He reached his hand to his throat.

It was over so quickly; she was surprised at herself. She'd been worried he would fight her off. Or that she wouldn't cut deep enough. Pausing before she climbed down off the bed, she took the blade and quickly scratched three little lines into each cheek. Bunny whiskers. Satisfied, she wiped the blade on the bed and closed it, sliding it back into its hiding spot.

She cleaned herself up in the bathroom, wiping him and the surfaces she'd touched down with alcohol wipes she'd packed in her bag.

She slipped out a side exit of the hotel unnoticed and disappeared into a dark alley, pulling off the mask and tucking it into her bag.

CHAPTER THREE

BUNNY WOKE up the next morning with a pep in her step that hadn't been there in ages. She'd been so jaded by the number of men telling her about the horrible things they either did or wanted to do.

She put on some music and started cleaning her apartment. She scrubbed the kitchen as though she had the energy of someone reborn. Weightless. Not carrying the burden of someone else's stories.

She shook, she shimmied, and she boogied her way through the deepest clean her apartment had ever had. The sheer joy seemed to flow from her fingertips as she scrubbed every nook and cranny.

Finally, she crashed on the couch, picking up her phone. A text message from her friend Bette made her smile. She wanted to go out to a club that night and dance. Bunny texted her to let her know she was in and then sat back to scroll her social media feed.

As she was scrolling, a breaking news article stopped her in her tracks. Her thumb poised above the phone. Some kind of fresh energy hummed just under her skin.

Something in her chest blossomed. Pride. She was proud of what she had done. The article was neutral, and the comment section was mostly filled with a mix of comments mentioning charitable things he'd done. But every few comments, a kernel of truth would pop up. *This perv likes little kids.* She scrolled down some more. *He paid for a 12-year-old to go on a private cruise with him. Wonder where he got the money for that. Gag.*

Those comments made her stomach twist. But they also made her feel like she'd done a service to the kids in the city. One less pig out there trying to buy what he wanted.

The Purple Room had a line streaming out of it. Hopefuls wanting to get into the club. The bouncer gave her a nod, and she slipped past the others standing in line, ignoring the "hey, she cut" comments.

"Thanks, Dylan." She smiled up at the bouncer as she slipped under his arm into the door. She made her way directly to the bar, and her friend, Sam, the bartender, glanced up and grinned. He poured her a drink, and she slid onto the barstool to chat with him for a minute while she waited for Bette.

"You look light and airy tonight."

"Maybe I finally lost something…" she answered vaguely. He quirked an eyebrow and opened his mouth to say something else, but an impatient customer at the other end of the bar shouted something to the tune of, "Stop flirting and get my drink!" so Sam shrugged and turned to help the others waiting.

Bunny sipped her drink, watching the TV behind her. A news clip interrupted the game that was on, and she froze. She couldn't hear what they were saying, but a picture of The Charity Man flashed by and then the outside of the hotel. A description of a "person of interest" popped up. The words 'rabbit head mask' made Bunny's throat tighten.

A guy a couple seats down was watching the TV. He loudly joked about some "Bunny Mask Killer," and then he slid his gaze over to Bunny.

"Hey, isn't your name Bunny?" His laughter was louder and longer than the joke deemed worthy. Bunny rolled her eyes.

"Dave, you're drunk," Sam said to the guy, who just laughed again.

Thank god for Sam sometimes. He'd come to her rescue too many times to count with perverts and assholes at the bar. It was how they'd become friends, and their connection was almost visceral. She'd never had a friend like him. He didn't *want* anything from her. She didn't know why, but she was grateful for it. He was a loner like her — and they needed each other.

Bunny turned her head away, busying herself with her drinking, scanning the club for Bette.

The drink suddenly burned her stomach — she hadn't expected them to have a description already. She was going to have to be a lot more careful about the mask. She wasn't the only sex worker who wore costumes or did roleplay, but she had to be careful not to fall into a trap. Everyone would be watching for a rabbit head mask soon.

Suddenly, she didn't want to think about anything. She signaled to Sam to pour her two shots of tequila. She sprinkled salt on her wrist and licked it off. Then she downed both shots quickly, biting the lemon slice he handed her and dropping it next to the glasses. She chased it with the rest of her drink and set the glass down, hopping down off the stool. Bette could come find her on the dance floor.

Right now, she needed to experience something else, to feel the press of the bodies on the dance floor jostling her, the sticky way her shoes stuck, the sour smell of the men on the dance floor whose pit stains on their shirts mingled with their beer breath, the heavy bass vibrating the floor, and the flash of the disco lights pulsing with the beat. Anything to distract her from that little pit of worry balling in her stomach.

CHAPTER FOUR

THE ROOM SMELLED of whiteboard markers and leather cleaner — faint, artificial, trying too hard to be sterile. He'd asked for a "classroom scene." Said it with a shy laugh over text, as though embarrassed by the cliché.

Bunny had smiled, and said of course. She could be anything — professor, principal, punishment. People were simple once you gave them a stage.

Now, seated on the edge of the desk in her short pleated skirt and knee-high socks, she watched him from behind half-lidded eyes. He was smaller than his messages. Sweaty. His collar too tight.

When he smiled, his teeth seemed to apologize for something they hadn't said yet.

"Have you been behaving, Mr. Donalds?" she purred. Somehow she knew the last name he'd given was real. He wanted the fantasy to be as real as possible.

He swallowed, nodding too fast. His hands trembled where they gripped the arms of the chair.

He tried to speak in character, mumbling about being a

"bad student." But his excitement made everything come out jagged, awkward.

The words hung between them like smoke. She corrected his posture, tapped the ruler against her palm.

"Bad students need to learn their lessons," she whispered, and his breath quickened.

There — a flicker.

When she said "students," his pupils widened in a way that made her stomach turn cold.

The word itself wasn't what excited him. It was the picture it painted behind his eyes. The connection to some real-life student… or students.

She stepped closer, the click of her chunky heels marking each second like a metronome.

He shifted in the chair, a small laugh bubbling up. Nervous. Childish.

"God, you're really good at this," he said, trying to lighten the moment.

But his voice cracked on the word "god," and she caught the edge of guilt beneath it. Bunny circled him once, slowly and deliberate.

She smelled the sourness of his fear then, the way people smell before they confess.

Her voice dropped. "Tell me something, Mr. Donalds. What do you think about when you're alone?"

He froze.

"I — uh —"

"Don't lie. Not to me."

The ruler pressed lightly against his cheek. Not hard enough to hurt — yet.

"Tell me," she whispered. "How young?"

He blinked, confused. "What — what do you mean?"

Her tone sharpened. "How young were they, when you first started looking?"

His mouth opened and closed. A fish out of water, drowning in the air. He tried to laugh it off, but the sound came out brittle.

"That's not — I don't — this isn't —" He flubbed his words.

Bunny slapped the ruler down on the desk beside his hand. The crack was so loud it seemed to split the air.

"Don't," she said. She was done playing.

Her posture straightened; something in her mind shifted. It was as if the rabbit mask was watching through her eyes now. Her mind flicked to it for just a minute, briefly wishing she had it with her.

He was stammering. "It's just — fantasy. Everyone has —"

"Fantasy doesn't leave bruises," she said.

Her voice was barely audible.

"Fantasy doesn't hide in staff rooms and parking lots."

His face paled. "You don't know what you're talking about."

"I do." She paused. "I always do."

For a moment, the silence felt alive — a small animal breathing between them.

Then she stepped back, slipping the ruler into her bag. The scene was over.

She didn't need to touch him. The fear was enough — for now.

He started to cry before she reached the door. Not loud sobs, but the quiet kind that sounded like a faucet dripping.

She turned once, watching him shake.

"Class is dismissed, Mr. Donalds." She turned and left.

Back in her apartment, she undressed and climbed into the scalding hot shower. She scrubbed at her skin until it was an angry pink. She remembered a time when her job hadn't made her feel this dirty. It had been fun then — she hadn't known anything about her tricks, and it had been good that way. In a way, she didn't want to know these things.

It was bad enough growing up in a house where her mother constantly brought home a new man — always a new man. Always one with more perverse predilections than the last.

The rabbit mask wanted to know. The rabbit mask seemed to beckon from the closet, calling to her.

"Fine, one more lesson," she said out loud, as if answering it.

CHAPTER FIVE

MORNING SMELLED of bleach and iron. She couldn't remember when she last slept. The sheets were speckled pink where she thought she'd washed everything clean.

Brush teeth. Wash hands. Scrub nails. Again. On repeat.

Bunny stood at the sink, scrubbing her fingernails. She'd gotten a little carried away, and the blood clung to her nail beds like ivy to a tree. The sink filled with rust-colored water, and she scrubbed harder. For a second, she thought she heard faint laughter coming from the pipes.

She froze. The sound stopped. Only her reflection moved. Her lips, the rabbit's smile. Squeezing her eyes shut tight, she looked in the mirror again. Just her, nothing unusual. She scrubbed her hands harder, making them raw.

When she was done, she examined the rabbit mask, feeling like it was watching her all the while. She cleaned it as best as she could and sprayed it liberally with disinfectant deodorizing fabric spray. Hanging it in her closet, she realized the entire closet was taking on that faint metallic scent.

We'll have to do something about that, she thought, her eyes connecting with the rabbit mask's eyes.

"Yes, we will." The mask sent its own message.

The days blended together. She couldn't remember what day yesterday was, or what the day before was.

She took appointments. She saw her regular tricks and new ones.

She ate. She showered. She slept. Maybe. She couldn't remember actually having slept.

She joked with Sam about the "rabbit killer mask" in the paper. He laughed, she laughed louder. But her laugh is hollow and dies abruptly. He gave her a weird look and then was called away by a customer.

Later, she thought about the joke again and laughed to herself. She didn't really know why.

I did good, she told herself out loud, wiping her blade. Examining the whiskers she'd scratched into her trick's face. Her trademark now.

We did good, something answered. It didn't sound like her voice — not exactly. It was higher, muffled, as if spoken through fur.

A candle-lit room. Red wax dripped, slow as syrup.

The businessman, her regular, calls her *Miss Rabbit* now — they all do.

He said, "You're famous, you know." Then he laughed, as if it was a joke. He didn't actually believe she was the infamous Rabbit Mask Killer.

She tilted her head, all innocence.

"Then smile for the camera," she said, but the flash never came.

Later, she watched his blood trace the cracks between floorboards, finding paths she didn't know existed. She wanted to follow.

White sheets in the washer, spinning, spinning, red thread winding through them. She stared at the glass until it looked like an eye — open, unblinking.

She whispered to it, "Tell me I'm still me."

The machine hummed back; *we are.*

She was walking home late at night. Neon lights blinked pink and blue across the puddles.

Someone catcalled her — a high, taunting whistle.

She turned her head slowly, the way prey never would.

The man faltered. Something in her gaze, something he couldn't put his finger on — made him cross the street. He scurried away, glancing over his shoulder.

She smiled into the glass window of a storefront. Her reflection's smile was wider, bigger.

Two rabbits now. One inside the other.

Bunny fiddled with her drink at the bar, her feet swinging on the barstool. She stared at herself in the mirror behind the bottles. Transfixed.

"Rough week?" Sam's voice interrupted her. She nodded.

"You wanna talk about it, babe?" he asked.

She turned her head slowly. Smiled. "I already did," she answered. He pulled his eyebrows together, confused. Opened his mouth to ask her a question, but a belligerent customer at the other end of the bar was shouting about needing another drink, so he reluctantly turned and walked away.

Night again. It was always night now. Maybe she slept during the day. She didn't know. She couldn't remember seeing the daylight.

She was lying in bed, and the rabbit mask sat at the foot. It whispered, "You can stop pretending now."

"I'm not pretending."

"Then why wear me at all?" it asked.

She didn't answer.

It was almost dawn; she was on her hands and knees scrubbing the floor. The tiles gleamed. Her hands shook. Exhausted.

Humming, she looked at her reflection in the oven window.

In the reflection, the rabbit mask hummed with her.

CHAPTER SIX

THE CITY TURNED her into a story. The rabbit mask was making a splash, overtaking headlines throughout the city.

She heard it everywhere now, threaded through ordinary noise — between the hiss of espresso machines, the slap of cab doors, the mutter of late-night strangers. The sensationalism of it — a female serial killer? A vigilante? These comments passed along from interaction to interaction — a kind of thrill, the way people talk about natural disasters about to hit.

"Did you hear? Another one. Scratches on the face, like claws."

"She's a vigilante. I'd buy her a drink." This comment made Bunny smile to herself.

"She's crazy. They always are."

Bunny listened from her usual seat at the bar, hair still damp from a shower. The faint scent of soap and bleach clung to her skin. The television above the counter looped the same footage she'd been avoiding all week — a blurred alley, police tape glowing under harsh light, a shadowed figure in the corner of the frame. For half a second, she'd thought she recognized her own posture. She took a slow sip of her vodka and cranberry, the ice clicking like small bones.

Sam polished glasses behind the bar, his hands moving without thought. "They're making her out to be a ghost story," he said, trying to sound casual.

Bunny smiled into her drink. "Aren't all women ghost stories eventually?"

He laughed, a small, uneasy sound, and changed the channel.

Online was worse.

Someone had posted her photograph, or someone who could be her, blurred into pixels and speculation. There were threads devoted to decoding her "pattern," to ranking her supposed victims by sin. A podcast called her "a mirror held to male guilt."

In clubs and backrooms, the whispers rippled through her world. Some of the girls were afraid; others sounded almost reverent.

"She's one of us," someone said, reapplying lipstick in a cracked mirror. "Maybe she's keeping the monsters in check."

Bunny turned her face away so they wouldn't see her smile. For a moment, she wanted nothing more than to confess — to spill the truth about everything. Sometimes she felt so alone.

But then — a message arrived. A new client, a blank profile picture — a white mask. The text was brief. *I want the killer experience.* She stared at the words for a long time before replying. Was this a trap? But she couldn't help herself. She responded. *Describe what you want.*

There had been a long pause — those flashing dots had her holding her breath until the message popped up. *Surprise me. I want to see what it feels like to be afraid of you.*

Something twisted low in her stomach — not anger, not thrill. Something she couldn't put her finger on.

The rented room smelled of cheap cleaner and sour gym socks. Wallpaper peeling in thin curls, a single lamp throwing everything into soft, dirty gold. She laid out her things on the bed — silk gloves, the restraints, the rabbit mask — but the blade stayed zipped in her mask.

When he knocked on the door, she slipped on the mask, adjusting it so that it sat firmly in place. Every time she put it on, it felt more and more like a second skin than a mask.

"You look like you could hurt someone," he said, laughing a little.

"Maybe I could," she answered. She didn't laugh back, and the smile dropped from his face.

The scene unfolded as they always did. Her movements were rehearsed, fear pretending to be fantasy. But when she lifted the rabbit head, and he flinched — not from terror but delight — she felt the air escape her.

"Do it," he breathed. "Be her."

But she couldn't do it. She lowered the mask, and told him the session was over. She didn't know if it's because he hadn't confessed the level of guilt she needed. Or if it's because she let the rabbit do the decision making when she had the mask on.

He left, confused and irritated, mumbling something about false advertising. She wasn't sure if he actually wanted to die, or if he was hoping she would push him to some limit and then let him go. She didn't even know if he realized *she* was *the* rabbit mask killer in the news.

There were apparently knock-offs now. Other workers were taking their role-play to new levels.

The silence after he was gone felt almost physical. She stared at her reflection in the mirror after scrubbing it clean. The rabbit mask lay on the bed behind her like another body. For the first time, she felt the hunger rising without its usual disguise of purpose. No justice, no lesson —just the need itself, raw and bright.

It frightened her more than any headline ever could.

She stepped back from the mirror, as if distance could undo what already stirred inside her. Outside, sirens wailed somewhere far away. She told herself they were for someone else. But in the darkened window, she swore she saw the rabbit's reflection tilt, just slightly, as if it was watching her.

CHAPTER SEVEN

THE NEED BUILT WITHIN HER. It took over her every thought. Every waking minute, she was thinking about the next man who deserves what he gets. She knew her perfect target.

John Rout. City politician. Untouchable. At least so far.

But Bunny knew John was also a client of one of the other workers she knew — Darla — a friend of sorts. At least someone she was friendly enough with that she was privy to some insider information.

So it wasn't hard to set him up. All it took was making sure she spent more time with Darla. She pretended to be getting closer to her. She needed every detail to be perfect. And Darla loved to talk about her tricks.

John. A regular. Every Tuesday morning. Same hotel, same hotel room. Same time every Tuesday. Without fail. All Bunny had to do was show up in Darla's place. Without her knowing.

So that's what she did. She didn't want to set Darla up, so she slipped her some sleeping pills and made sure she passed out with her bedroom door wide open. She had roommates who would be up and see her sleeping. Not to mention, the apartment she lived in had lobby cameras that would record her going in but not coming out. An alibi.

John was surprised when someone other than Darla walked in. A mix of confusion and excitement passed over him like a wave, and Bunny smiled to herself. She had the mask in her bag, but she didn't need to wear it today. This one was for herself.

"You've been a naughty man, and I'm here to punish you." She waved a small hand whip back and forth playfully. John chuckled and leaned back on his elbows.

"Oh, you think I've been naughty, do you?"

It took everything in Bunny not to just rush forward and slash his throat right then. The pompous ass. She knew all of his disgusting affinities. "The younger the better" could have been his motto.

But Bunny couldn't let her emotions control the situation, or the situation would control her. No, she had to remain rock steady.

"I know you have. I'm sure you have. Tell me about it," she said as she knelt in front of him and undid his belt, unzipping his pants and tugging them down.

He laughed, almost wheezing as he shifted to let her pull his pants down around his ankles. He talked, telling her horrible things he had done to women and *girls* who were "not dirty whores" like her. *Good one,* she thought and rolled her eyes.

Reaching toward her bag, she slipped her hand in and pulled out a few things.

"Let's just shut you up. Less talking, eh?" she said, making sure her voice was whispery soft. She wrapped the mask around his face, popping the ball gag in his mouth.

He reached up as though to resist, but she moved his hands away from it with one hand as she stroked him with the other. He watched her intently, and leaned back on his elbows again, his eyes growing wider.

He reached one hand up to cup her breast. "Uh uh uh" — she wagged her finger at him — "I do the touching." She reached down where she had dropped a pair of soft handcuffs.

She clamped them around his wrists before he had the chance to object. Not that he could say much anymore. He made a noise in his throat. Fear. She could smell it on him. He realized maybe he wasn't so untouchable. But the fear was still laced with fantasy.

His eyes registered how vulnerable he had made himself. No doubt he thought about what he would do if she left him like this. There was no part of him that imagined he wouldn't walk out of that room, though. No, he was thinking about how he would have to call one of his lackeys to free him from the cuffs and gag. His eyes scanned the room. *Probably checking to see where he left his cell phone.* She could read all of these things just by the way his jaw tightened, his eyes creased, and how he licked his lips.

Bunny stepped back for a moment, just watching him. He stared at her hungrily, his phone and escape forgotten. She reached up and cupped her breast, as she squatted down to retrieve the last item she'd pulled from her bag. The one he hadn't even noticed.

Her switchblade.

She flicked it out, and for a second he thought it was part of the game. The upturn of his eyes, lift of an eyebrow, and she had known he wasn't scared enough yet. But her entire demeanor changed, and she no longer moved sensually. Her movements became calculated. She meant business now. She debated for a minute about making this one extra special. *I could cut off his dick. Replace the ball gag with it.* She wondered if that was the rabbit head's idea or hers, but then shrugged and took the first step.

His eyes bugged out of his head; blood spurted out over his legs as she held up her prized possession. He struggled to get his hands free, and almost instinctively she reached out and slashed his throat open.

She'd become so practiced at this part that she knew how far to step back to avoid most of the blood spray. She pushed his shoulder so he would slump backward on the bed rather than forward, falling off.

Bunny waited for the blood flow to slow. Until his glassy eyes stared at the ceiling, devoid of life. Then she unhooked and peeled off the ball gag as she slipped her trophy in its place. *There.* She left his hands cuffed.

She stepped back, appraising her work. Proud of herself. Her eyes flicked to her bag on the floor and she wondered if the rabbit head was proud of her too. Or upset that she'd gone solo.

As she cleaned herself up, she hummed a lullaby to herself. The silence was unbearable. She thought about what she'd done.

She didn't feel the same sense of justice as she had with the others. But she didn't have time to dwell on that; she just had to get home and scrub herself clean. So that's what she did.

CHAPTER EIGHT

BUNNY ADJUSTED her mask before entering. She'd been suspicious of this trick for a while, but he was quiet. He didn't blurt everything out as if he were bragging. Like the others.

"Hi Bunny," he mumbled as she entered the motel room. He was sitting on the bed, his button-down shirt untucked, sleeves rolled up. But otherwise still fully dressed, everything in place.

"Hello Mark." She set her bag down on the armchair next to the bed and sat on the bed next to him.

He closed his eyes and waited. She crawled up on the bed, kneeling behind him, and ran her fingernails down his back. But he immediately noticed a difference.

"Your nails are shorter." He craned his neck as if he'd be able to see behind him. Bunny looked down at her fingernails. Rusty red stains around the cuticles. She'd had to cut them all short to keep them clean. But the stains just wouldn't go completely away.

"Yeah, sorry," she said, shrugging. "Tell me about your deepest fantasies, Mark." She felt impatient. He shifted uncomfortably. She didn't want to play this cat-and-mouse game of coyly pretending to be into the sickness so she could get a confession. She just wanted to jump right to that part so she could serve justice.

"Umm," he stuttered, laughing awkwardly. She pressed her fingers into his back, urging him to continue. Leaning forward, she whispered in his ear. "I just want to know your darkest, dirtiest details, Mark. I want to know every single inch of you." She let the fur of the rabbit mask brush his ear, and he shivered, a low moan humming in his throat.

"There's a girl," he said, but paused. Bunny ran her hands up and down his arms and leaned forward so that her nipples trailed up and down his back.

"Tell me," she insisted.

And he did. He told her about his co-worker's daughter. He didn't know how old she was, but he heard her talking about starting middle school, so Bunny knew she must be only around ten or eleven.

She was glad he couldn't see her face. Sometimes hiding behind the rabbit mask was a necessity. The tears that pricked at her eyes were real. She was once that little girl. She barely heard what he said; the anger had blossomed in her.

His voice trembled with something that sounded like remorse.

"But I've never…." His voice broke. She wanted to believe him. But the rabbit whispered, "He's lying." And the little girl. Even if he hadn't… it didn't mean he wouldn't.

"You're sick. You're fucking sick. Why would you even think about that? Some little… kid?" she spat at him, the rage suddenly exploding. Mark twisted around, confused.

She didn't remember climbing off the bed and getting to her feet, but suddenly she was standing right in front of him, her hand pressing his chest to force him to sit back down.

"But I didn't do anything, Bunny. I've never..."

"Shut up," she said, reaching up at her mask, sliding her blade out. "Sick fuck." She hissed as she plunged the blade into his chest, pulling it back out. "You didn't yet, but you *wanted* to." She stabbed again. He tried to block the knife, but she stabbed at his hands too.

"Bunny!"

She lost all sense of reality — she didn't know how many times she stabbed him. She'd never stabbed any of the victims. Usually, she just cut their throats clean across and carved whiskers on their faces. Everything prior had been clean. Articulate. Careful. Calculated.

She was covered in blood. Her mask, her body, head to toe. She had never been this clumsy. This messy. This emotional. This desperate.

When it was over, she sat on the floor, wrenching the rabbit head off, dropping it next to her. She released a stream of loud uncontrollable sobs. Realizing she had killed an innocent man. One with a disgusting fantasy, but the first who hadn't acted on it.

"I'm sorry," she whispered, gulping loudly.

No one heard. Mark's body was slumped back on the blood-soaked bed, glassy eyes staring blindly at the ceiling.

CHAPTER NINE

BUNNY LAY IN BED, staring at the TV. She watched as the banner ran across the news broadcast, with a description of the "rabbit mask killer."

A grainy image of her in the rabbit head popped up. It had only been a matter of time before some surveillance camera caught her image — and now she had to worry about where and when she might have put the mask on or taken it off. What images might be floating around of her without it.

Eventually, someone would recognize her.

A knock at the door made her entire body tense up. *They're already here for me,* she briefly thought but jumped out of bed in her oversized t-shirt and went to peer through the peephole.

Sam.

What was Sam doing here? Sam didn't just drop by unannounced.

"Bun, I know you're in there," he said, but his voice was soft and buttery. She immediately reached up and unlocked the deadbolt, twisting the knob to open the door.

"Hey," she greeted him and stepped aside as he breezed past her. She stood back while his eyes roamed her small apartment. Looking for clues? She didn't know, but he had a certain look. Kind of wild, mostly concerned.

"Are you doing okay? I haven't seen you around for a couple days, and you haven't answered my texts." Sam wasn't clingy, but she also usually checked in regularly.

"Sorry, yeah, I'm okay." Her voice was quiet as a mouse, and he just looked at her. "Do you want something to drink? I could make a pot of coffee or…" She let the sentence hang in the air, waiting for a response.

"Okay, sure." His watchful eyes followed her across the room. "Can I use your bathroom?" he asked, and she nodded without thinking as she measured out the coffee beans.

A minute later, Sam reappeared in the kitchen holding the rabbit head mask between two fingers, his arm out as far away from his body as he could get it.

The coffee mug Bunny was holding slipped out of her fingers, clattering to the kitchen tile, pieces of ceramic skittering every which way. She blinked, unsure of what to say, squeezing her eyes shut and pressing her fingers against her eyelids.

"You could've told me," Sam said, setting the mask down on the floor like the tainted object it was and moving to help clean up the broken mug pieces.

Bunny didn't know what to say for a long time. Sam didn't seem surprised or appalled at all. He seemed sad, worry etching his eyes. And maybe a bit heartbroken that Bunny had been keeping secrets.

"I was teaching lessons," she told him.

"What kind of lessons end like this?" His voice was soft.

Sam knew her past. Her whole history — he was one of the few. So he knew why she ended up like this.

Mostly. She would never say out loud what she believed. The mask had given her some kind of power to do all of this. She couldn't have done it alone. Wouldn't have.

"I'm sorry, Sam." Her voice broke, face crumbling as she dissolved into tears. He held out his arms, and she fell into them, letting him comfort and soothe her.

"You have to stop, though. You're going to get caught," Sam finally said as she pulled back and reached for a box of tissues to blow her nose.

"I know." She nodded, and then sighed loudly, as she glanced over at the mask. It was disgusting at this point. It smelled horrific. The white fur was matted and stained. Although she tried to freshen it up and clean it after every session, there was only so much she could do.

"We should burn it," Sam suggested as he followed her gaze.

Something inside Bunny shifted. She felt, more than heard, the other voice. *No, you need me.*

"Yeah, okay. Let's do that," Bunny answered Sam, her voice barely above a whisper.

And they do. They had to take the mask to Sam's small house so they could use his fire pit to do it. Bunny watched as the mask melted into a disgusting, matted mess and finally into ash.

"Thanks, Sam." Bunny forced a tight smile as he dropped her back off at her apartment. He patted her knee and gave her a sad look.

"I'll see you at the bar this week?" he asked, but something in his voice betrayed him. They both know he wouldn't.

Bunny swallowed hard, forcing the lump in her throat to go away. "Sure." She pressed a kiss to his cheek and jogged up the path to her own apartment.

Bunny packed a duffel bag full of essentials. She turned on her cell phone and jotted down a couple of phone numbers, shoving the list in her wallet. Just in case. She lingered on her collection of vinyl records, on her stack of books, on her huge collection of costumes.

All replaceable, Bunny reminded herself. She pulled out the box from under her bed. Sorted through the stacks of cash, shoving them into the pocket of her duffle bag. She thought about her bank account and decided she wouldn't worry about the meager balance in it. She would leave it.

When she was done, she stood at her door, looking around her small apartment that had been home for so long. She ached with longing. All things considered, this home was the one she'd been the happiest — the free-est she'd ever been. Setting her key on the kitchen table, she locked the door and left. She'd already scheduled an email to send to her landlord in a week. She felt bad that he'd have to have the apartment emptied and cleaned out, but she knew she didn't have options.

On the way to the bus station, she stopped next to a trash can. Before tossing her cell phone in, she powered it down, and then set it on the sidewalk and stomped on it with her boot heel. Picking up the pieces, she tossed them in the trash and continued on.

She bought her bus ticket with cash, but she knew it

was still a risk, because there was no way to board without her ID. She got on and found a seat, and stared out the window at the darkening night as the lights of the city disappeared in the distance.

Goodbye east coast.

CHAPTER TEN

DETECTIVE O'HARA

DETECTIVE JACK O'HARA sat alone in the incident room, the yellow lamplight turning the papers on her desk the color of old bones. Midnight crept across the city outside, brushing its neon fingers against the station windows. She had long since grown used to these hours — courting exhaustion as though it were an old lover — but tonight fatigue made her hands unsteady.

There were too many notes, and not enough. She flipped open the thin gray folder again, the one marked UNSUB 14B — "Rabbit" in her handwriting.

Over the past three months, seven men had turned up dead in ways that suggested skill but not indulgence. The eighth possible link was messier — it seemed personal in a way the others hadn't. Or someone attempting to be a copycat?

Her signature was the scratched whiskers on their faces.

The suspect — a figure in a rabbit-headed mask, seen only once, moving like a shadow slipping out of frame.

Witnesses described the person as slight, quick, and —

most tellingly — wearing the kind of platform heels favored in the strip clubs. A sex worker, possibly. Maybe by choice, maybe just by cover. Jack tapped a pen on the edge of the file.

The victims weren't sympathetic men. That much was clear. Misuse of charity funds, accusations of trafficking and child abuse. The list went on, each name dirtier than the last. But a common theme was child sexual abuse.

If Jack had been a different sort of detective — the kind who pretended justice was a tidy thing — she would've ignored that pattern. But years on the force had taught her the world leaned unevenly, and some people only fell when they were pushed.

Still, vigilante or not, a killer was a killer. And Jack had a job.

She leaned back, stretching her aching shoulders as she sifted through her observations from the last crime scene. The Rabbit's precision. Nearly-sterile removal of physical traces. The way she — no, the suspect — entered and exited locations like she'd practiced for years.

Jack rubbed her temples. "You're getting sloppy, Rabbit," she murmured, gazing at a photo of the last victim's alley. A single heel print had been left in the grime. Too clean. Too unguarded. It felt intentional. A message. Then her phone buzzed.

Detective Dom Reyes, night shift liaison, had texted: Lead on the mask girl. Tipster claims your suspect goes by 'Bunny' at The Purple Room. Last seen a week or two back. Got an address. Witness says they saw someone go into the apartment about an hour ago.

Jack's breath hitched. She had chased ghosts for weeks; now, one finally left a footprint. She grabbed her coat.

The apartment building was nicer than Jack had expected — a quaint little building buried in a trendy neighborhood. Jack climbed the bright stairwell. Apartment 3C waited at the end of the hall, door slightly ajar.

Never a good sign.

She paused, one hand on her weapon, and nudged the door open with her foot. The place was quiet. Too quiet for someone who'd left in a hurry — no TV glow, no heater hum. She stood in the doorway, making note of every detail. This was what she was good at.

The living room smelled faintly of cleaner and coffee. A coffee mug sat on the coffee table, rim stained red from cheap lipstick. But everything else felt… staged. As if Bunny — or whoever she really was — had erased herself with care.

Jack scanned the room. No signs of struggle. No bloodstains. No overturned furniture. But the absence of chaos was itself a clue. A sudden noise from the bedroom made her freeze. "Police! Come out with your hands up," Jack shouted, holding her weapon steady.

A little old man scurried out of the bedroom, a heaping trash bag dragging behind him.

"Wh-what's going on?" he asked.

"Who are you?" Jack demanded.

"I'm the landlord here — Gary Withers — doing a clean out. What are you doing here?" he said, his hands still lifted.

"When did this tenant leave?"

"I couldn't say for sure — but I got an email yesterday that she had moved on. What's this all about?"

"I'm investigating a case —"

"Do you have a search warrant?" the landlord asked, suddenly more confident.

"No — but it won't take long to get one," Jack admitted.

The landlord shifted back and forth, and finally shrugged.

"Okay, sure, have at it. The tenant said she was gone but couldn't take the rest of her stuff. She left me the key. You can have a look around."

Jack nodded, putting her weapon back in its holster.

She moved with careful steps, her eyes sweeping everything. The kitchen drawers were all open. Empty. Cabinets too. The refrigerator hummed but held nothing but a half-empty bottle of water and a wilted lemon. Jack crouched and checked behind it. Dust. No hidden stash.

"How much of this did you clean out and how much was gone when you got here?" she asked, gesturing toward the kitchen cabinets and drawers.

"That's what's in the trash bag… Seems like the tenant left almost everything. You wouldn't even know she moved out."

Jack nodded and stepped past the landlord into the bedroom he'd just come out of.

A small vanity hosted an array of cheap perfumes and foundation compacts — some cracked, others mysterious shades that couldn't match any single face. She opened the top drawer and found a bundle of receipts from costume shops, wig boutiques, thrift stores. The dates spanned months. A woman of many faces. But none of them included the rabbit.

Jack turned to the closet. She hesitated only a second before sliding the door open. A wave of fabric spilled into the dim light — silk slips, vinyl bodysuits, sequined dresses in shades that glimmered like spilled gasoline. Dozens of heels lined the floor, some towering, some modest. A feathered mask hung at the back. A fox. A wolf. A painted porcelain face like an opera ghost. But no rabbit head.

"Of course," Jack whispered. She stepped further inside, running her hand over a red velvet coat. The air smelled faintly of sweat, talc, and something metallic. Her stomach tightened. She knew that scent. You smelled it sometimes even after a crime scene had been scrubbed. Blood had a memory stronger than bleach.

Jack stepped back out of the closet. Something wasn't right. Not wrong, just… unfinished. On the bedside table, half-hidden under a folded scarf, she noticed a small notebook. Black cover, elastic band. She pulled it free and flipped it open. The handwriting was inconsistent — some entries flowing, others jagged, hurried.

"They don't stop unless someone stops them."

"He followed the girl out the back door again. Tonight? Or wait for proof?"

"Mask keeps them guessing. Keeps them afraid."

Jack's pulse slowed as she turned each page. Nothing was explicit. Nothing that could stand in court. But intent radiated from those pencil strokes like heat.

And then one entry, dated ten days ago:

"Someone is watching me. Time to disappear before she puts the pieces together. Not ready to face her yet."

Her breath caught.

Her?

Jack sat on the edge of the bed, absorbing the words. The Rabbit Mask Killer had known Jack was closing in. Or at least someone was.

Had she been watching Jack in return? Tracking her

investigations? Jack remembered the heel print again. Too clean. Too deliberate.

Had the message been meant for the police — or meant for her?

For a moment, a strange, unwelcome thrill curled in Jack's chest. Curiosity. Admiration, even. A woman who carved justice into men who'd slipped through the cracks — Jack understood that impulse better than she wanted to admit.

But understanding wasn't permission.

She snapped the notebook shut and stood.

A full forensic sweep could reveal blood traces. Fiber matches. DNA if she was lucky. But she hesitated, fingers brushing the notebook as though it might burn her.

Pursue the vigilante, and she might save a life.

But stop the vigilante, and she might condemn the next victim to a system that had already failed them.

For the first time in a long while, Jack felt truly uncertain.

She tucked the notebook into an evidence bag, then paused at the threshold of the bedroom, giving the room one last, lingering look.

"Where'd you go, Rabbit?" she murmured.

The silence didn't answer. But she had the faintest sense — like a shift in air pressure — that someone was listening.

She closed the door gently behind her, as if not to wake a sleeping ghost.

EPILOGUE

BUNNY STOOD in front of the bathroom mirror, studying her reflection as if it were a stranger she might have to kill. She tilted her chin, examining the way the cheap overhead bulb carved shadows along the planes of her face. The faintest smirk ghosted across her lips.

A sharp exhale fluttered her new bangs, making them dance like nervous insects.

"Not bad," she murmured to the empty apartment.

She'd never worn bangs before. Too girlish, too soft, too *not her*. But this was a new city. New home. New rules. A new look to slip into like a fresh skin.

She picked up the scissors again, their metal grips still warm from her last pass, and reached behind her head. The sound — *shnk, shnk* — echoed in the narrow bathroom, each snip a tiny rebirth. Strands drifted down her neck, tickling her collarbone before settling at her feet.

A mullet. A spunky little thing. All sharp edges. The way she felt inside.

It felt right.

It felt like this city — rough in the back, business in the

front, and trying too hard to pretend it wasn't dangerous in every direction.

In the mirror behind her, she caught a sliver of the small bedroom. The place was nicer than the last one — nicer floors, at least — but half the size. A shoebox with ambitions.

She'd picked up a few necessities: a skillet that already looked like it had trauma, a mismatched set of plates, a cheap toothbrush, sheets that smelled like someone else's memories. Enough to say someone lived here. Not enough to say who.

Her gaze drifted to the bed, to the mask she'd laid in the center like a shrine offering.

The kitten head stared back at her with big, unblinking eyes — cute, harmless, sweet.

Another lie with whiskers.

She walked toward it slowly, the floor creaking beneath her bare feet. The kitten's glossy pink mouth curled up in a permanent smile.

Purrrr, it seemed to whisper.

Not mocking. Welcoming.

She reached out and traced the edge of its jaw. Smooth. Innocent.

Not like the rabbit mask she'd left behind in the old city.

The one she'd burned.

The one they were still looking for.

The kitten was a fresh page.

A new beginning. And maybe an end for someone else.

Bunny lifted the mask, feeling its weight settle into her palms, light but full of promise. The city beyond the window hummed its night song — sirens, shouting, the low rumble of something violent but familiar. A place ready to be played with.

She smiled at her reflection in the dark glass.

"Let's see what trouble we can find," she whispered to the kitten.

And the kitten smiled back.

JACK RABBIT

SARA LEA

CHAPTER ONE

THE CITY HAS a way of forgetting its monsters. Rain slicks the alleys clean, headlines shift to fresher tragedies, and the public attention span—already thinner than one-ply toilet paper—moves on without a backward glance. But I don't forget. Not the mask. Not the crime scenes. And certainly not that feeling that clung to me long after the files were boxed up and stamped inactive.

Officially, the Bunny Mask Killer hasn't been seen in four months. Unofficially—my reality—Bunny never left.

I'm sitting in the dim corner of the precinct archive room, lit only by a dimming desk lamp that buzzes like it holds a grudge. Everyone else went home hours ago, but I stayed, breathing in the dust like it's giving life.

My laptop glows with an open browser tab. A news clip from three states away. **Second Murder in Two Weeks. Police Searching for Suspect in Animal Mask.**

I hit play again. The footage is grainy—someone's cheap phone camera—but the silhouette is unmistakable. A woman stepping out of an alley, wearing a kitten mask. Not a bunny. A kitten. But something in her posture, in that slow, deliberate turn of her head toward the camera, in the way she tilts like she's listening to something only she can hear—it hits a nerve.

I pause the video and lean in. The woman's shoulders—narrow, tense. Her hands—relaxed, fingers slightly curled. Her stillness. Her control. All of it echoes the killer I was tracking four months ago. Here. In my own city. With the few surveillance photos and small video clips, it's hard to be sure. But I *feel* sure. Call it years of experience. Call it gut instinct. Call it whatever you want.

Admiration.

I close my eyes, and the memory rises with painful clarity. I'd missed her by days. By the time my trail had come close enough, she'd packed up and left the city. Run like a scared rabbit. Or a smart one.

I force my eyes open and shove the memory aside. Maybe this video is a coincidence—a copycat, a thrill seeker, a creep with internet access and no impulse control. Morbid fandom grows online like fungus. We'd seen a string of copycats after the real Bunny had left. They'd been easy to spot. Messier. And no signature. They'd eventually died down. But something in me knows this is no copycat. It keeps tugging at me. Invading my sleep.

I play the clip again. Searching for any other clues. I can't pinpoint exactly why I know it's her. I just do.

My jaw tightens. If she isn't Bunny, she's studied her. Maybe even knew her.

I pause the video, rub my eyes, and remind myself this isn't my case anymore. Bunny vanished, the department moved on, and Captain Ruiz told me—first nicely, then not—to let it go. But I can't. Bunny isn't a ghost. She's a habit threaded deep in my nerves.

I close the video and scroll through the comments—an

always-terrible choice, but irresistible. People argue over whether the suspect is hot, psycho, or some deranged feminist icon. Then one comment snags my attention: **Same woman from the Baxter case?** I go still. Someone else saw it.

The account is newly made. Blank. A burner, meant to drop a single clue and disappear. My fingers move before my conscience can weigh in, as I enter their PD website. Case details. Male victim, mid-thirties, on the sex offender registry. Killed with one precise cut to the throat. Whiskers carved into his cheeks. Kitten whiskers, they speculate. But I know the truth. Bunny whiskers. My breath leaves me slowly. There are countless ways to kill a person, but this is no coincidence. The signature was never made public.

The clock reads 2:41 AM. I should go home. I should sleep. Instead, I replay the clip. The masked woman steps out again, tilting her head with that eerie, unhurried awareness. For a moment—maybe a glitch, maybe not—it feels like she's looking straight into the lens. Straight at me.

I slam the laptop shut. This is how Bunny worked her way into my head before—through the quiet moments, through the cracks in logic. She made me think about morality with a clarity that made you feel blind by comparison. I hated how persuasive she was, without even trying. Hated that some part of me agreed with what she was doing.

"Don't admire her," I mutter. "She kills people." But admiration isn't something I can simply turn off.

I pack up and leave the archive room. The hallway lights flicker, making my shadow sway along the floor. The building hums with after-hours emptiness, amplifying every small sound.

Just as I reach the exit, my phone buzzes. Unknown number. No caller ID. My throat tightens.

I answer.

Silence stretches. Then—a voice, soft and unmistakably familiar. Almost gentle.

"Detective O'Hara."

My pulse slams in my ears.

Bunny.

"It's been a while," she says. "You've been looking for me."

I freeze, gripping the phone. "Where are you?" My voice sounds rough, stripped bare.

A brief, thoughtful pause. Then: "You're watching the wrong city."

The line goes dead.

I stare at the black screen, breath thin. I don't question the call. I don't doubt the message. Bunny didn't disappear. She stepped out of frame.

And now she wants me to follow.

CHAPTER TWO

CAPTAIN RUIZ'S office always smells faintly of burnt coffee and accumulated frustration. I linger in the doorway for a moment, steadying myself before I knock. I came straight from my apartment—no sleep, just a scalding shower and the grainy footage running in loops behind my eyelids.

Ruiz glances up from a stack of reports and raises his brows in that familiar what now expression. "O'Hara, you look like hell."

"Morning to you too." I step inside, closing the door behind me. "I need five minutes."

"I don't do five-minute miracles before coffee."

"This isn't a miracle." I place my laptop on his desk and flip it open. "It's a lead."

He sighs but sits back, signaling for me to continue. I cue up the video. Even muted, it radiates tension—the masked woman emerging from the alley, the unsettling tilt of the kitten head.

Ruiz rubs the bridge of his nose. "Is this from some horror movie?"

"Local news. Their local PD uploaded it last night." I play it again. "Look at her stance. Her hands. The way she turns her head. Tell me that isn't familiar."

He watches with strained patience, the kind reserved for an appliance that's about to break. When the video ends, he closes the laptop gently, as if sudden movement might trigger me.

"Jack," he begins, voice firm. "We're not doing this."

"She called me last night."

That stops him. "She called you?"

I nod. "Blocked number. She told me I was watching the wrong city."

He leans back, expression tightening. "Are you sure it wasn't a prank? You've been deep in this case for months."

"I know it was her," I say, too quickly, too intensely. I calm myself. "I know it."

Ruiz drums his fingers on the desk. "We closed that case. FBI has the interstate angles. We don't have jurisdiction there."

"She's not there," I keep my face as blank as possible. "That's what she meant. The footage is connected. Either she did it, or someone who studied her did."

He gives me a look that's equal parts sympathy and annoyance. "We're not chasing ghosts across state lines. Not for a maybe, not for a hunch, and not for a killer who vanished four months ago."

The bluntness stings, but I keep my gaze locked on his. If I show doubt, the conversation ends.

"She's not a ghost," I tell him. "She's active. She's changing. And she reached out to me."

Ruiz snorts. "Because you made yourself reachable. You've been wound tight over this case from the beginning. Hell, people even have a nickname for you."

My jaw tightens. "Oh?"

"Jack Rabbit," he says, almost kindly. "Because you chase every trail, no matter how many traps people warn you about."

The nickname crawls under my skin. Rabbits run blindly. I don't. I follow patterns, signals. It's a logical chase.

"This isn't running," I say. "It's doing my job."

"No," he corrects. "Your job is the stack of assault cases you're ignoring while watching grainy footage at two in the morning."

I swallow the flare of frustration. "Just let me make one call to their PD. Cross-check the case details. If I'm wrong, I'll let it go."

"You won't," he says simply. "And that's the problem."

Silence settles, thick enough to choke on. Something inside me tightens—duty on one side and that darker pull, the one Bunny left embedded under my skin, on the other.

Ruiz stands and walks to the window, watching the morning shift shuffle across the parking lot. When he turns back, his face has hardened with decision. "You need time off."

I blink. "What? No."

"Yes." His tone is final. "A week. Minimum. Recharge. Reset. And stay away from Bunny."

"I'm not burned out," I deny.

"You look it."

"I'm not."

"O'Hara—"

"Then give me a few days off," I cut in quickly. "I'll get distance. I just need to clear my head. Visit my aunt. She's been sick."

He pauses. "Your aunt?"

I nod, keeping my face smooth and unreadable. I don't talk about family, so he can't call me on the lie. But I don't flinch.

Ruiz studies me, weighing options. Let me stay here and obsess, or send me away and hope I come back steadier? Finally, he sighs. "Fine. Three days. But you check in. And you do not take your badge across state lines for anything related to this."

"I won't," I say.

He lifts an eyebrow. "Say it like you mean it."

"I won't. I promise."

He doesn't believe me. Not fully. But he lets it go. "Go home. Eat. Sleep. And stay off this case."

"Understood."

I turn to leave. Something holds me still for a breath too long, something tight and unspoken. Ruiz softens slightly. "Jack Rabbit," he says quietly. "Stop setting traps you fall into."

I give him a brittle smile. "Wouldn't dream of it."

When I walk out, it feels like shedding a layer of civility with each step. The bullpen hums with the ordinary chaos of the morning shift—phones ringing, paperwork shuffling, someone laughing too loudly. None of it touches me.

At my desk, I open the drawer and stare at my badge and service weapon. Taking them would raise questions. After a moment of consideration, I slip the badge in my pocket, closing and locking the drawer with my service weapon inside. Instead, I lift my notebook and a thin folder of photocopied Bunny case materials—the ones I'm not supposed to have.

Outside, the air is crisp, the early sun glinting off windshields. A familiar hum runs through me—the one that wakes up whenever I'm close to something dangerous, when instinct sharpens into purpose.

I lied to my captain without blinking. I'm leaving the city. I'm following the faint trail Bunny left, whether she intended it or not. She wants to be understood—that much has always been clear.

I'm beginning to understand her. Slowly. Uneasily. And worse, I'm starting to believe she understands me too.

I slide into my car. The radio crackles, flickering to static for half a second—barely noticeable. But the hair on the back of my neck rises.

I shake it off and pull out of the lot. I tell myself this is just following a lead. I tell myself this is still about justice.

But underneath all of that is a truth I can't outrun.

I'm not chasing Bunny. I'm being invited.

And Jack Rabbit is already running.

CHAPTER THREE

I DON'T KNOW where she is, but I go anyway. The longer I think about it—her telling me I'm looking in the wrong spot is sure to be an attempt to mislead me. It means I'm looking in the right spot.

I drive overnight without stopping. As I enter the streets of this new city—so unfamiliar to me—a sense of unease grows. I'm used to knowing the ins and outs of every street and neighborhood in my precinct. Feeling lost is a new sensation for me. I don't like it.

I roll my window down, feeling the energy of this city —a slow roll of humidity fills the car. It smells like tarmac and cigarette smoke. My GPS directs me to the extended-stay motel I found. Not coincidentally, two blocks from the grainy video footage. I slow as I pass that alley, recognizing the neon sign for the bodega below it.

The parking garage I find nearby is questionable, but I take my chances. It's close. And right now, convenience is everything. Being on a case like this—I have a one-track mind. And this case; it's personal now. I would never have admitted it to Ruiz, but it is. Deeply.

Checking in at the motel, I quickly drop off my duffel bag and head back out. I don't stop to worry about when they last washed the duvet (if ever), or to check to see if they cleaned the bathroom. No, I do none of that. Despite not having had any sleep and having survived off cups of coffee and gas station snacks, I get to work immediately.

I stroll down the block, pretending to mind my business, but anytime one of the girls walking up and down the street stopped and leaned into the window of a car, I took my opportunity to observe her. I'd ruled them all out. No, Bunny wouldn't be out here walking the street. I knew that, but I also knew I couldn't ever miss a possibility. New city—maybe Bunny had trouble picking up high-end clients here.

Then again, probably not. She was too smart not to have figured out her 'in' the minute she arrived.

I stop walking when I reach the alley she'd been caught walking down. A quick glance up and I spot the city's surveillance camera. Not hidden at all. Bunny had to have known it was there. I don't glance up at it when I pass, like she did though. Instead, I tuck my chin in the other way and slip through the door of the bodega.

The store is not busy. Feels lucky, like I'm meant to be here right now. I approach the guy behind the cashier.

"Hey," I say, keeping my tone light, tired-traveler neutral. "You work the evening shift normally?"

The cashier doesn't answer right away. He's a lean guy in his mid-twenties, eyes sharp in that way that tells me he's learned to clock danger before it clocks him. He wipes down the counter with a frayed towel, buying himself time.

"Why?" he asks finally.

"I'm looking for someone." I tap the counter once, a

soft metronome to steady his nerves. "Girl. Short. Wavy blonde hair. Wears a kitten mask sometimes."

His eyes flicker—too fast for a civilian, not fast enough for someone truly hardened. He knows something. Or he's scared of something. Both help me.

"Never seen her," he answers.

Lie. I lean in, just slightly, letting him see I'm not here to shake him down. I'm here because I'm not leaving without answers.

"She walked down your alley," I say. "Last week."

His jaw tightens. That's my confirmation. But I don't push. Not here, not yet. People in cities like this don't spill their guts—they leak them slowly, through cracks you pry open with patience.

I thank him anyway, step back out, and hit the sidewalk.

The street workers clock me instantly—not as a threat, but as something out of place. Wrong shoes, wrong posture. A woman alone who isn't selling, isn't buying, isn't lost. They read me accurately. Cop energy. Even out of state, even out of jurisdiction, it bleeds off me like heat.

A woman in a pink wig and boots up to her thighs gives me a long, assessing look. I approach her because she's the only one not pretending she hasn't noticed me.

"Evening," I say.

She snorts. "Hmm."

"I'm looking for a girl. Wears a kitten mask."

The reaction is subtle but unmistakable—a shift of her weight, a small swallow, her gaze sliding past me to the alley like she expects someone to be listening.

"You a cop?"

"Not here," I shift my weight from one foot to the other. "Just looking for someone who's in trouble."

She studies me again, slower this time. Then she jerks her chin toward the alley. "Lot of girls in trouble down there."

"But this one puts other people in trouble," I say. "Fast. Precise. Chooses them, doesn't stumble into them."

Her eyes sharpen. "Yeah. Heard of her. People call her… Kitten Head Killer. Kind of an urban myth. Some say she's bad news. Some say she keeps worse guys from creeping around. I can't be mad at that. As a woman. Or out here, on the street, doing what I do."

Fear and admiration wrapped tight together. That's Bunny. That's always been Bunny.

"You seen her?"

"No." She hesitates. "But some folks have. Girls who work in the salon. The businessmen from Highview Towers." She tips her chin. I follow her gaze to the skyscraper. No surprise. Probably full of high-end businessmen and politicians with dirty secrets.

I thank her, then move on.

I pass a guy at a makeshift station stuffed between a tattoo shop and a laundromat—folding chairs, stacks of electronics tucked behind his table.

When he notices me, he straightens. Wariness first, then curiosity.

"You lookin for something?" he asks.

"No," I say. "Someone."

"Oh?" he asks, too casually.

I keep my expression still. "Yeah. Maybe you've seen her. Woman in a kitten head mask?"

He glances around, then lowers his voice. "Heard about the aftermath of one of her last week. Guy twice her size, built like a refrigerator."

Target selection. Controlled force. She's telling me a

story in the bodies she leaves behind. A pattern. Almost like choreography. A dance I've stepped into.

"Any idea why?"

He shakes his head. "No clue. But she doesn't hit random. That's what scares people. If she chooses you? Means she knows something. Must have been one bad dude."

I nod slowly. That tracks. Bunny never did anything without meaning. Even her chaos was calculated.

I step back from the table, heart hammering now—not with fear, but with recognition. A rhythm. The edges of her pattern clicking into place. She's hunting someone new right now.

I glance toward the alley again. The walls seem to pulse, like they're holding their breath. My breath catches with them.

"She's still here," I whisper to myself. "Has to be."

And if she knows I've arrived?

Then she's already waiting for me.

CHAPTER FOUR

THE NEIGHBORHOOD I'm staying at is on the edge of the industrial district, which sits on the edge of the city like a forgotten limb—rows of metal warehouses, shuttered factories, and lots where rusting machinery slumps like old war veterans. Light traffic. The hum of power lines and the intermittent screech of tires occasionally play in the background.

If Bunny's here, she isn't hiding. She's watching.

I pull the collar of my jacket up as I move between the hulking silhouettes of the buildings. The streetlamps are sparse, creating tall shadows in the alleys as the darkness of the night closes in.

The lead I'm following came from a call into the local PD—someone reported "a woman in a kitten mask arguing with a man in a service alley." No officers responded. Too understaffed. Too used to bullshit calls.

I'm not.

The alley behind Warehouse 54 is longer than it looked on the map—narrow, cluttered with old rotting pallets, and graffiti layered so thick, the paint peels in chunks.

I scan for a hint of anything. Blood, scraps of clothing, the metallic tang of violence. Nothing fresh.

Halfway down the alley, I hear movement. I know it's not Bunny. It's too loud. Too careless.

Three men step out from behind a dumpster, blocking the exit. They've got that posture street predators get—the overconfidence of people who've only ever fought prey.

"Well look at this," the biggest one drawls. "Tourist hour?"

I ignore him and keep walking, slow and steady. They close in. Of course they do.

"Hey," the second one says, stepping directly into my path, blocking me. "You lost, sweetheart?"

Wrong word. Wrong tone. Wrong day.

"I'm working," I say.

"Oh yeah?" He laughs. "Doing what?"

"Finding someone."

"Yeah? Maybe we can help."

I'm two seconds from putting him on the ground when I feel the cold press of metal against my spine.

Gun.

Sloppy placement. Too high. Amateur.

"Let's see your bag," the man behind me orders.

I breathe once. Fine.

I raise my hands slowly and shift just enough for my jacket to fall open—revealing the badge clipped inside. Not my jurisdiction, but street rats don't read jurisdiction.

The one with the gun freezes. The others tense.

"Shit," the big one mutters.

"You want to think really carefully," I say softly, "about what you do next."

There's a beat where no one breathes. Then the gun

pulls back. They scatter like cockroaches yanked into the light. Within seconds, I'm alone again.

I let out a slow breath. My pulse thuds once, hard, then settles. I tuck the badge out of sight and continue toward the end of the alley.

That's when I see him.

A man sitting on an overturned bucket, back pressed to the wall, shaking so violently his teeth chatter. He's older —fifties maybe—and thin in the way that suggests long-term struggle, not sudden trauma. His eyes dart up as I approach, wide and wild.

"I'm not here to hurt you," I say.

He laughs—a broken sound. "Don't matter. She'll be back anyway."

My heart jolts. "Who?"

He lifts a trembling hand and traces an invisible curve in the air. "The kitten girl."

I crouch down. "Tell me what you saw."

He swallows hard. His voice drops to a whisper like he's afraid the walls might tell on him. "Not saw. Heard. The man she grabbed… he begged. Not for his life. For forgiveness." Another swallow. "That's what made it worse."

"What did she do to him?"

"Dunno. Didn't follow. Wouldn't." His eyes lift to mine, sharp with a sudden, startling clarity. "Everyone thinks she's saving people. That she protects girls, or punishes creeps, or whatever story makes 'em sleep better."

I brace myself.

"But that girl?" His voice fractures. "She don't save people. She punishes monsters."

My breath leaves me in one steady exhale. The words reverberate in my brain. *Punishes monsters.*

It's exactly what Bunny was doing. Her victims weren't random. They were chosen. Curated. She'd left messages not in ink or blood, but in the lives she ended.

"What changed?" I ask. "Why is everyone suddenly afraid?"

He leans in, whispering like the shadows themselves might eavesdrop. "Because she ain't just hunting monsters no more."

A chill spreads down my spine.

"She's escalating," he says. "She's becoming one."

For a moment, the industrial yard feels too quiet. Too expectant. Like she's just out of sight—listening.

And for the first time since I hit this city, I'm not wondering if this woman is Bunny.

I'm wondering what she's become now.

CHAPTER FIVE

THE FIRST SIRENS start blasting into the night as I make my way through the industrial corridor—soft at first, then rising with the layered echoes that bounce between the warehouse walls like trapped birds.

They carry a sense of urgency I recognize too easily. Out here, where most businesses have died and the city's infrastructure moves on autopilot, police presence is usually inconsistent at best.

When sirens arrive quickly, it means someone important made the call or someone frightened enough pushed past the apathy that they normally encounter.

I keep my pace steady, adjusting the collar of my jacket against the damp air drifting between the alleys. The whole place smells faintly of rust and wet concrete, the kind of heavy industrial scent that clings to your lungs whether you want it to or not.

As the sirens swell and gather somewhere ahead, their lights begin to flicker against the distant sheet metal—a fragmented, jittering dance of red and blue that throws warped reflections across the empty windows.

For a moment, the district feels like it's waking up, moving toward the commotion even though its heart stopped beating a decade ago. Police lights do that in dead neighborhoods; they act like defibrillators, jolting the area into a parody of life.

When I reach the corner of the next warehouse, the scene begins to take shape. Two squad cars have angled themselves haphazardly across the loading zone, their doors still open, engines idling. Officers move quickly but not with confidence—more like people who've walked into a room they sensed was dangerous but cannot yet see why. Their postures are tight, shoulders raised, hands near holsters or flashlights. Whatever the initial call said, the reality in front of them is escalating beyond it.

I stay in the shadows for a moment longer. An out-of-state detective lingering at a crime scene with no official capacity is one question away from becoming a suspect or an obstruction, and right now I need information more than legality. The trick is to approach slowly, with the vaguely cautious curiosity of a passerby who cannot help rubbernecking but has no intention of stepping over the police tape. My body falls easily into that posture—it's one I've mimicked often enough during deep-cover surveillance.

And then I see him.

The man is on the ground near a stack of wooden pallets, his body positioned at a harsh angle. He's hog-tied with hardware zip ties thick enough to secure fencing, the plastic biting into his skin but not cutting through it. When one of the officers raises his flashlight to take a closer look, the beam catches the curvature of his jaw, the specific shape of his nose, and recognition snaps into place. I hear him mumble the victim's name to his partner. Seth "Stunner" Maddox.

A sex trafficker with a network that snakes through multiple states, notorious for slipping out of indictments and investigations like he's greased in baby oil. Every time someone gets close to cornering him, he evaporates—the case collapses under suspicious circumstances, or a witness recants, or evidence vanishes.

The justice system treats him like a mirage. Visible long enough to acknowledge but never solid enough to grasp. Slippery little fucker. And yet now he's here, discarded like the trash he is.

Not killed. Not even unconscious. Alive and breathing, though each breath sounds labored and unsteady.

I step slightly closer, positioning myself behind a column of crates to avoid catching the officers' attention. From here, I can see his chest more clearly—smears of blood, sweat, and grime covering his skin. The markings carved there are deliberate, shallow enough to avoid major bleeding but deep enough that they won't disappear quickly. Three thin arcs branch outward from near his sternum, shaped with steady precision. The lines are unmistakably meant to resemble whiskers. Longer than the bunny whiskers that were carved on the faces of the victims back home. Her signature. But bigger. More sure of herself. This is not the work of someone copying her.

The officers nearby begin to murmur. One of them curses under his breath, mumbling about it being Maddox, and another lifts his radio to report in a voice tinged with disbelief. Their confusion fills the space with a nervous buzz, a static of uncertainty that only amplifies the tension.

A paramedic kneels beside Maddox, cutting the zip ties carefully. The sound of the shears closing around the plastic is sharp, unnervingly final. Maddox tries to lift his head, fails, and lets out a hoarse, broken noise that is less a word than a reflexive plea.

Fear has made this sleazy ferret of a man into a puddle. Not fear of the officers. Not fear of the legal consequences. Fear of her—of the one who left him like this, stripped of his power, of his untouchable reputation.

I feel a subtle shift in the air around me, a prickle along my skin that has nothing to do with the night breeze. It's the sensation of being observed—closely, deliberately—by someone who knows how to stay just beyond sight. I lift my gaze toward the rooftops in a movement slow enough not to draw attention.

The buildings loom above, silent and severe, their silhouettes jagged against the dull glow of distant city lights. I scan each ledge, each metal platform, each darkened window where a curtain might shift. There's no visible figure, no sudden motion, nothing I can point to and name.

And yet I just know it. She's there. Watching. I can feel her eyes on me as strongly as I would the caress of a hand.

The awareness grows stronger the longer I stand still, like a thread being pulled taut between us. It's not hostile, not exactly. It's observational, curious, and tinged with something that feels almost like satisfaction.

As if she's pleased I found the scene. As if she wanted me to witness Maddox like this—to see what she's capable of when she's operating without the constraints she used to follow. Like a cat bringing their owner a mouse and saying, "See what I brought you? I did this."

It's a message not just for Maddox, but for me.

I should feel revulsion at the sight of him. Or anger. Or sorrow. Something clean and morally grounded. But instead, an uncomfortable truth stirs low in my chest—an acknowledgment of the twisted relief that someone finally stopped him, even if the means fall far outside the law.

The legal system failed the women he trafficked; Bunny didn't. That realization unsettles me more than anything else, because it blurs lines I've spent my whole career enforcing. It tempts me to accept a version of justice I know I shouldn't.

The sensation of being studied deepens, almost as though she can read my thoughts.

I step back, retreating into the darker part of the alley where the officers cannot see me. My footsteps sound too loud against the concrete, though I know they're light.

The moment I turn away, the invisible attention tracking me sharpens, then gradually recedes, like a presence withdrawing into the night. Only when the sensation fully dissolves do I allow myself to exhale, the breath long and measured, my pulse still unsettled.

This is no longer the Bunny I chased months ago. That woman was consistent in her principles, rigid in her rituals, her kills defined by deliberate intent. This version is bolder, running on a new philosophy she hasn't shared yet but is clearly ready to demonstrate.

She's not just stumbling on targets now. She's hunting them with a precision that is terrifying.

She's changing. And whatever transformation she's undergoing, she intends for me to witness it.

The question, as always, isn't whether I should follow. It's whether part of me has already started doing so without meaning to.

CHAPTER SIX

I SPEND the next day in bed, searching online chats for hints or comments about where Bunny might be. One particular place is mentioned several times. So when evening closes in, and the street lamps come on, I make my way out.

I stop in front of the Velvet Hook, though nothing about it is velvet and the only thing hooking people is desperation. The neon sign outside flickers in sickly pink pulses, buzzing loud enough to be heard over the hum of the industrial fans bolted to the roof. I stand across the street for a full minute before crossing—enough time to watch two men leave through the side door, collars up, faces blank with practiced denial.

Inside, the air is thick and warm, saturated with perfume, sweat. The floors are sticky from spilled liquor. Red bulbs cast everything in low, bloody hues. Conversations around me buzz like bees in a hive. It's not a place where people look for the police. It's a place where the police come to look away.

Most heads don't turn when I walk in, but the ones that

do are intense—assessing me. Checking to see if I'm a threat or an opportunity. I keep my posture relaxed as I approach the bar, shoulders loose, chin slightly dipped. I'm here for information, not fear.

The bartender, a muscular woman with two long braids and a gaze that could cut through glass, wipes down the counter. She doesn't ask what I want; she asks who I am.

"You new?" she asks.

"Passing through."

"Honey, nobody 'passes through' the Velvet Hook." She narrows her eyes. "You a cop?"

"Not tonight." I offer a thin, tired smile. "I'm looking for someone."

That gets a reaction—one she hides fast. "Everyone here is looking for someone."

"Not like this," I say. "Blonde. Short. Wears a kitten mask."

The bartender pauses, the glass she's polishing freezing in mid-air. She lifts her chin toward a hallway in the back. "Try the Rose Lounge. Girls who work the late shifts talk more than I do."

She slides a drink toward me without asking—soda water with lime. A quiet sign I'm walking where I shouldn't but she's choosing not to throw me out.

I nod once. *Thanks.*

The Rose Lounge is misnamed; it smells more like cigarettes trapped in thick curtains and too many spilled secrets. A pair of women sit on a couch under a string of dying LED lights, half-dressed, half-awake, fully aware.

I approach slowly, hands visible.

"I'm not here for trouble," I tell them. "I just want to ask about the woman in the kitten mask."

The one with short coppery-orange curls snorts. "Which one? Girls put on weird shit all the time for customers."

"She wasn't here for customers."

That makes them both hesitate.

The second woman, older, with long black shaggy hair and steady eyes, tilts her head. "What do you want with her?"

"I'm trying to understand what she's doing."

A small laugh. "Nobody understands her."

"She does," I say. "That's enough."

They exchange a look—a silent conversation as they decide how much to tell me. Finally, the older one gestures to the spot beside her. I sit.

"She wasn't here for work," she says. "But she watched. Listened." She taps her temple. "You could see she took notes in her head."

"For what?"

"For men," she replies easily. Too easily. "The ones who came through trying to spend money they shouldn't have. Ones who buy girls because they can't handle women." She shrugs. "We told her things because she didn't ask the kind of questions cops ask. She asked… smarter ones."

"Like what?"

"'Who scares you?'" she says. "'Whose name makes the other girls go quiet?' Stuff like that." She smirks. "You ever ask those questions, Detective?"

I don't answer. But for a moment, I reflect on that—my job is to serve justice. But sometimes I know we are just raking over the coals—picking and choosing, but never actually looking for victims. We wait until the victims find us to do anything.

Her smile softens into something almost sad. "She

wasn't afraid of them. Not the way we are." She taps her fingers against her thigh. "But she wasn't showing off either. She just... had some sort of mission."

The copper-haired one finally speaks. "She never gave a real name. We called her Kitten. Or Mask Girl. She didn't care." A pause. "She came back last night."

My pulse kicks. "Last night? Why?"

She shrugs. "Said she needed to say goodbye."

Cold floods my chest. "Goodbye to who?"

"Anyone who helped her." She looks me dead in the eyes. "Said she wasn't coming back here. That she was moving 'closer.' Whatever that means."

Closer to who? Or what?

The older woman leans forward until her knee touches mine, voice dropping to a whisper gentle enough to bruise.

"So," the woman finishes, leaning back, "if you're here to find her, honey... you're late."

I stand slowly, pulse sharp, vision narrowing.

When I exit The Velvet Hook, the night air slaps me with damp coolness.

For the first time since I arrived in this city, I feel exposed—as if she peeled back my ribs and peeked in.

She's planning something.

She's circling me. I find myself looking over my shoulder more. Feeling watched.

Somewhere in this sprawling city, Bunny—or whatever she's become—is smiling in the dark, knowing I'm exactly where she wanted me.

Not chasing.

Following.

Invited. A certain feeling rolls through my body—I can't exactly put my finger on it. The cat and mouse game feels different suddenly. Less violent. Sensual almost. It's almost as though Bunny wants to impress me with her own version of justice.

I'd be lying if I said it wasn't working.

I'd be lying if I said I wasn't turned on.

CHAPTER SEVEN

I SLEEP TOO LATE. The kind of sleep that isn't rest, just a heavy blackout—the mind shutting off because it doesn't know how else to protect itself. When I surface, sunlight bleeds around the cheap motel curtains in sickly yellow slants. My mouth tastes like metal. My body feels hollow.

When I check my phone, I'm surprised by the text message from an unknown number.

If you want the truth, come alone. 10PM. Behind Warehouse 18.

I stare at the screen until the words become blurry. Excitement zips through me. Undeniable—electric and sharp. But that feeling is quickly followed by dread—slower, like thick sludge crawling up my spine. A third feeling wiggling at the back of my mind.

A longing I can't explain.

I spend the day pacing my tiny hotel room—the musty smell and anticipation making eating undesirable. I check the time repeatedly, like the day is suddenly going to evaporate and I'll be late. I scarf down a candy bar from the vending machine before heading out.

Warehouse 18 is on the back of the industrial district, abandoned, near collapsing. The night air is foggy, and for the first time I feel naked and exposed without my sidearm. At 9:58, I stop directly in front of the warehouse's loading dock, looking up like she's going to rappel off the roof.

At 10:00, she steps out of the fog silently like she had made herself invisible until that precise moment. The kitten head mask is the first visible part, catching the faint glow of a streetlamp two alleys down. Then the rest of her —her small but solid frame, ash blonde curls poking out of the bottom of the mask.

She walks toward me, slowly and deliberately, before stopping about six feet away.

"Jaqueline O'Hara," she says, her voice sliding into my skin like a hook. Warm, with a slight tremor that would be undetectable to the average observer.

"Jack," I correct, and she tilts her head, the kitten, unblinking.

"Jack." A slight nod, before she starts circling me. Slowly, like a lioness circling her next meal. The circle gets smaller—not touching, but close enough that I can feel her body heat threading into mine.

"Why the mask?" I ask, forcing my voice steady even when my pulse is spiking. "I know who you are."

"It's not for hiding." She drifts behind me, almost sounding annoyed. Like I missed something. "It's for clarity."

"What clarity?"

"That you see me better when I'm like this."

She's not wrong. The mask removes the human softness, the vulnerability. Or transfers the vulnerability to me. Or her victims. My stomach knots.

"Is this where you kill me?" I ask. She stops circling, turning to face me head-on.

"No, this is where you finally understand."

"Understand what you're doing? It's murder."

"You've seen the men I choose, Jack. You know what they've done."

"That isn't your job."

"The system doesn't protect girls like the ones I meet." Her voice cracks—this is personal. "You know that. You've watched cases die out because of money or status or some old boys' club ate them up, made them disappear."

My chest tightens. She's right. I've lived all of that—a part of my job that I avoid thinking about because it would keep me up at night.

"You think killing them is justice?" I ask, my voice flat—devoid of judgment.

"I think letting them keep walking is cruel. Criminal even," she whispers, stepping closer. "I do it so they can't hurt anyone again."

"And what about you? What are you turning into?" I ask.

Her shoulders rise, then fall heavily. The quiet grows so strong, I almost don't want to breathe.

"I'm becoming exactly what I need to be."

"And dragging me along with you?"

She laughs softly, pain ingrained in the sound. "Jack, you're following me because you want to."

My heart hammers in my chest. "No."

"You came all this way. Does your captain know you're here?"

I swallowed hard, my eyes flicking away for a second.

The fog curls around her ankles like smoke.

"Seeing you chase me… it excites me." Her voice trembles under the mask. My knees weaken, heat inching up my spine.

"You shouldn't say that," I choke out.

"But it's true." She exhales deeply. "You make me feel seen. Alive." She pauses, a note of regret slipping into her voice. "And that's dangerous. For both of us."

She stops circling me and stands in front of me.

"Why did you ask me to meet you here?"

Her chest rises. "Because I need you to know what comes next."

"Why? What comes next?"

She steps closer until the toes of her boots meet mine. The world falls away, the fog, the dilapidated buildings, all of it. Only the whisper of her voice is real.

"I'm going after men worse than Maddox."

"And you expect me to do what? Help you? Prevent you?"

"No." She shakes her head. "Don't stop me."

Silent crashes between us like waves at high tide.

"I can't promise that."

"You already have. By showing up here." She lifts a hand to my face, but doesn't touch me. The heat from her hand radiates, warms my jaw as she lowers her thumb to my bottom lip. Slides it over, gently, lovingly.

"You want the truth, Jack?"

"Tell me," I breathe, my chest hitching.

Her entire posture changes. The real Bunny. Still under that mask somewhere. Vulnerable. Hurt. Her voice breaks me.

"I'm doing this because someone has to. And because

knowing you're behind me—even when you shouldn't be, makes me feel braver."

She pulls her hand away, and I struggle not to follow. She steps away.

"But that's not the only truth," she admits.

My breath catches. "Then what else?"

Under the mask, I sense she's smiling, and I hear it in her answer.

"That I want you to follow me. More than I should."

She turns and walks away, disappearing into the fog, one slow step at a time, like she's dissolving into the night as easily as she appeared. It's as if she knows I'll follow.

And the terrible part?

It's like my feet and body betray every sense of logic.

I'm already moving.

CHAPTER EIGHT

THE FOG SWALLOWS her shape until only the faintest silhouette remains—a pale outline, dissolving and reforming with each breath of cold air rolling in from the bay. For a second, I think she's gone.

Then she stops. "Jack." And waits for me.

I take a step forward, then another. When I'm close enough to see her outline again, she lifts her hands up, removing the kitten head.

It's a simple act, unceremonious. But it feels like a punch to the throat. My throat strangles itself as I will myself to breathe, to swallow.

Her face emerges, hardened in the angles, but fragile in a softness that takes me by surprise. Strong cheekbones, but a rounded face. The ash blonde curls spill out of the mask, seeming endless. A small scar near her mouth. Gentle eyes, that don't match what she's done. What she's become.

Beautiful. Not like a glamour model—not artificially. Beautiful in that quiet way. Almost ethereal. It doesn't fit with these ugly warehouses and alleys. And crime scenes.

My throat constricts as I regain the ability to swallow, to breathe without forcing it. Everything inside me tightens. She sees my reaction. Knows.

Her mouth moves into a curve—not a smile, but something else—like a hint of recognition.

"You shouldn't look at me like that," she whispers.

"I can't help it." And it's true. The Jacqueline O'Hara of six months ago would hate this version of me. Hate the way emotion, admiration... attraction, are all making fast haste of any sort of common sense, logic, or virtue.

Her lashes lower, like she's trying to shield something. Her own reaction, her own tremble. But I see it. I feel it.

Professional paralysis roots me to the concrete. Every instinct I've ever sharpened tells me to step back, to reclaim distance, to remember badges and laws and lines.

But I don't move.

"You wanted the truth, so here it is."

"What led you down this path, Bunny?" I force my voice out.

Her jaw tightens. A reflex— she didn't expect my question. Not here, not now.

There's a flicker—pain glinting through her eyes before she shutters it. She looks away, breath stuttering once. I watch her walls rise, fast and practiced.

"Don't." Her voice is a warning, closing down the softness I'd just seen.

"I need to know."

"You don't." She steps back, spine straightening, shoulders squaring, retreating inward.

"Bunny," I press, gentler. "What happened to you?"

For a moment—just a beat—she cracks. I see it in the tightening of her throat, in the faint tremor in her fingers still clutching the mask at her side.

"My past is not for you," she says finally. But her voice isn't cold yet. Not fully. "It's the reason I do what I do. The reason I won't stop."

"Did someone—"

"Don't." This time it's as sharp as a blade drawn too fast.

I swallow down my questions. The silence stretches between us.

Then she exhales, and the cold slides back into her posture—deliberate, defensive, absolute.

"I won't talk about who I was," she murmurs. "Because she's gone. And she needed to be gone for me to survive."

I step toward her once. Just one step. "Let me help you."

She shakes her head, slowly. Regretfully.

"You can't help me, Jack. You can only follow me. Or stop me. There's no middle ground."

"I don't want to stop you," I admit. "Not like this. Not tonight."

The confession hangs between us, heavy, pulsing and dangerous.

Her eyes soften again—an ache so unbearably human flickers across her face.

"That's exactly why you should," she whispers. "The closer you get, the more likely you go down with me."

The warning is intimate. Tender. And final.

Before I can speak—before I can make any decision, she steps backward into the fog.

"Bunny—"

She raises a hand. "Don't follow me tonight," she says. "Not yet."

Then she turns and is gone.

I stand alone behind Warehouse 18, my breath shaking for a long time. The world coming back to me one piece at a time. The buildings. The oily smell. The loud fans running. Suddenly, I'm acutely aware of where I am, in the middle of the night.

I stare after her for a long time, trying to clear my mind. I know I shouldn't be here. But it takes everything in me to will myself to turn and go back to the motel.

CHAPTER NINE

MORNING DOESN'T COME GENTLY. It drags itself into my motel room like an unwanted guest—too bright, too loud, too real. I wake with my cheek pressed against the scratchy bedspread, muscles locked in knots that feel years older than I am. My phone says 11:42 AM. I should feel rested after the hours I slept, but instead I feel hollowed out. Used up. Haunted.

Bunny's words still cling to my skin.

The closer you get, the more likely you go down with me.

I sit up slowly, pressing my palms to my eyes. I tell myself to stay focused. But my pulse betrays me, thudding rapidly at the memory of her face—beautiful in a way that doesn't belong in alleys or crime scenes. Or inside my thoughts.

I can't chase that. Not right now. Not today.

Today, I need answers. So I pull out the copied file of Bunny's case. The one I'm not supposed to have—and begin scanning the pages again. Her birth name. School records. Half-completed entries from Child Protective

Services. A handful of reports, all thin and unsatisfying, like the system documented her without actually seeing her.

A name stands out from one of the old files: Margo Langford, social worker. The handwriting beside her name is rushed, as if she scribbled it right before having to turn it in to her supervisor.

I grab my phone before I can talk myself out of it. The first number I try is disconnected. The second sends me to a voicemail so old the recording crackles with static. On the third attempt, someone finally answers.

"Margo Langford speaking."

The voice is older—raspy, weary, but steady. I hesitate, because I suddenly feel like I'm trespassing somewhere personal.

"Ms. Langford, my name is Detective Jacqueline O'Hara. I'm calling about—"

"I know who you're calling about," she interrupts, voice tightening. "I wondered when someone would finally reach out again."

The "again" lands like a weight.

"I'd appreciate anything you can share," I say carefully. Silence hums across the line—long enough that I think she might hang up.

"I remember her," Langford says, gently—in a way that makes my throat sting. "Hard to forget a girl who flinched at the sound of footsteps behind her."

My hand closes into a fist around the bedding.

"Stepfather?" I ask quietly, flipping pages of her notes.

A sigh. "Yes. And more than one foster home that should've lost their licenses long before she arrived. She was bounced around like a problem instead of a child. Sadly, she was never the problem."

I shut my eyes. I can almost see it. Bunny, younger. Smaller. Clutching a cheap backpack from one placement to the next. Waiting for someone to recognize danger before it swallowed her whole.

"She begged me once," Langford continues, "not to put her in another mixed placement. Said she didn't want any men near her door at night. She was—"

Her voice wavers, the memory breaking something in her.

"She was terrified."

My breath leaves me, slow and uneven. I think of Bunny last night—her voice trembling under the mask, her confession cracking open through her defenses for a moment so brief and painful I almost missed it. *I won't talk about who I was… because she's gone.*

"What happened to her after that?" I ask.

"She turned seventeen and signed herself out of the system as soon as she legally could," Langford says. "And the day she left… she was crying, but she still thanked me."

That does it. The wall I've been desperately keeping up inside myself fractures straight down the middle.

"Ms. Langford," I manage, voice rough, "do you think she was dangerous? Back then?"

"No," she says immediately. "She wasn't a danger to anyone. She was just… waiting for someone to believe her. To protect her." A pause. "But I worried who she'd become if nobody ever did."

The words settle into me like stones.

We both go quiet.

Eventually Langford asks, "Why now? Why are you looking for her?"

Because I need to understand her.

Because I can't stop thinking about her.

Because last night she warned me away with a kind of tenderness I'm not sure I deserve.

Because she's not just a killer—she's the product of every system that failed to shield her from the monsters she now hunts.

Which response to give? I settle on something close to true.

"Because she's in danger," I say. "And I think she thinks she's alone."

Langford exhales, slow and sad.

"She always thought she was alone, Detective. Even when she wasn't."

We thank each other. She hangs up.

Silence fills the room.

I drop the phone onto the bed and lean back against the peeling headboard. My chest tightens, heat gathering behind my ribs, spreading through me like guilt, like grief, like something sharp and new that I don't want to examine too closely.

This changes everything. And nothing. Because I knew. I've always known.

Bunny isn't simply a killer.

She's someone the world abandoned until she adapted in the only way she knew how. Someone who learned to survive by becoming the very thing she feared. And the worst part? I don't feel further from her after hearing it. I feel closer. Too close.

Close enough to start understanding her logic, her hunger, her choices. Close enough to feel the ground shifting under my feet, tilting me toward something I can't justify and can't walk away from.

I press my palms to my face and whisper into the darkness of my hands. "What the hell are you doing, Jack?"

No answer comes. Just the hum of the motel heating system and the pulse that still jumps when I think of her face in the fog, saying *I want you to follow me.*

And god help me—

I want to. More than anything.

CHAPTER TEN

A CERTAIN TYPE of emptiness fills me. A feeling I'm unfamiliar with—a longingness for something I don't have in my life. Love. Partnership. Family. What's only ever been a fleeting thought, sits heavily on me today. Weighing down more and more as each minute passes.

The ache gets so strong that I get dressed and force myself to leave the motel room—even though I don't have any leads to chase today.

I spend the evening walking the streets, eating street vendor food, and stopping at shops. I don't ask a lot of questions.

The feeling that something binds me to Bunny burns in the back of my mind. It's like a string drawing us together.

Dusk is setting when I find myself near the industrial corridor again. It's as though my feet have a mind of their own. The sounds of some sort of scuffle a couple of alleys away make me freeze in my tracks. My ears strain to make sense of what I'm hearing.

The grunts and sounds of bodies struggling against each other intensify, and then suddenly an *oomph* followed by a wet sucking sound. I slip into the shadows, quickening my pace. As I get closer to the sound, a man comes bolting out of the alley. He doesn't see me, but I see him, and the faint light catches the glint of the knife in his hand.

Somehow I know before I even see her. I know the string is pulling me in for a reason. I step around the dumpster in the alley and Bunny is slumped on the ground, leaning against the warehouse.

I let out an involuntary cry. A reaction I'm not prone to.

Bunny is hunched forward, hand pressed to her leg. Her hand is covered in blood, and I realize the stabbing sound was her. Being stabbed. Not doing the stabbing.

I drop to my knees, and reach out for her. She flinches, trembling as she moves away.

"Bunny, it's me. It's Jack," I say softly, my voice barely a whisper.

She looks up from under her lashes, eyes wet.

"Let me help you," I say. She doesn't respond but keeps herself protectively angled away from me.

"Bunny, come on. Let me." I place my hand on her other leg, slowly and gently. Barely making contact. She doesn't flinch. I peel off my jacket and then slip the long sleeved t-shirt I have on over my head. Her eyes flick up to me for a moment, but I'm not even considering the fact that I'm sitting out in an alley in my bra.

Until her eyes graze over me, pausing to make eye contact. I feel the flush building up my chest and neck, until my cheeks are burning.

I lean forward and gently move her skirt aside. She's wearing boots just above the knee and a poofy skirt that just barely meets the boots. He managed to stab her right above her knee. I wrap the shirt around her leg, pulling it tight and pressing down. She winces.

I realize how close we are when I glance up and her face is inches from mine.

"Are you okay? The blood seems to be slowing," I choke out. Fortunately, it doesn't look like the cut is nearly as deep as I'd thought at first.

"It's okay, I've had worse pain." Her voice is soft but flat—devoid of the emotion that she can't hide in her eyes. She doesn't move away from me and I can feel the heat from her breath on my face.

She licks her lips and I force myself to look away. I shouldn't be thinking what I'm thinking. Not about her. Especially not right now. I focus on her wound.

"We need to get you cleaned up." I stand and slip my jacket on, zipping it up as I suddenly realize how chilly the air is. "Do you think you can stand?"

"Of course, yeah," Bunny says and clumsily gets up. She reaches over and grabs the kitten head mask from the ground. I hadn't realized it was there. I wonder if she took it off or if it was knocked off during the fight, but I don't ask.

"Where are staying? Is it close?" I ask.

"Yeah, I stay in one of the units at the end of this block." She nods her head in the direction I came from. I slip an arm under her. She manages to limp along, grimacing with each step.

As we exit the industrial corridor, she indicates a building on the corner. It's a big building that looks like it was once an old library or some type of government office.

"Here?" I ask, eyebrow raised.

"Yeah, they have converted space for rent here." She shrugs and I let her lead the way.

At the door, she pulls an access card from her pocket and scans us in. We slip inside and I'm shocked at how modern and well kept the inside is. It's certainly miles above the motel I'm staying at. She leads me to the elevator and again scans us in. We ride up to the eighth floor and when we step out, I realize there is only one apartment on this floor.

She uses her card to unlock her door and we stumble together inside her apartment. It's sparsely furnished, but clean and well maintained.

Bunny limps toward a door, her bedroom I presume. When I don't follow, she pauses and turns back to look at me. "Are you coming?" she says softly, and I follow.

She walks through the bedroom and I glance over at the bed. She leads the way into a large master bathroom.

"I think I just need to soak this. It doesn't seem that deep." She gestures to her thigh, and I nod. "We both need to get washed up." She looks pointedly at me, and I glance down at the blood on my hands.

"Okay." I unzip my jacket and let it fall to the floor as I slip out of my boots.

She turns toward the bathtub and starts the water. Digging around in a small cabinet, she finds some epsom salts and throws a generous amount in the tub.

I'm watching her like it's the most fascinating thing I've ever seen. And maybe it is. She's mesmerizing in a way she shouldn't be.

She peels off her own jacket, dropping it on the floor. She starts to lean down to unzip her boots, but winces. "Can you… do you mind?" she asks quietly.

"Oh, of course." I squat down, sliding the zipper down on each boot and helping her step out. It shouldn't be sensual. Not with my bloody t-shirt tied around one thigh. But it is. I swallow hard.

She pulls her top over her head, her curls falling

around her bare shoulders. She reaches behind her and unzips her skirt, letting it fall to the ground. We stand there for a minute while the tub is filling. She's wearing a hot pink bra with matching panties. She holds my eye contact as she reaches behind and unhooks her bra, letting it fall down her arms and onto the floor.

I force myself to turn away, to force down the thoughts running through my mind. I move to the sink, turning the water on and pumping soap into my hands, scrubbing at the blood vigorously. Ignoring her movements behind me, although I can see them in the mirror in front of me.

When I glance up, she catches my eye in the mirror as she slips her panties down and steps out of them. I force myself to stare into the sink.

"You could wash up in the tub too." She beckons, and a jolt zings down my spine. I turn the sink off but don't move.

"Jack, it's okay," she says, and my shoulders relax. I turn around as she removes the shirt from her thigh and gingerly steps into the tub, lowering herself in. I'm relieved to see the bleeding has stopped. She hisses as the water washes over her thigh but then relaxes back against the tub.

I undo my pants, kicking them off, and peel off my socks. I haven't been in my bra and underwear in front of anyone other than at the gym in years. If she only knew how opposite we were in this aspect. She doesn't take her eyes off me, and I force myself to calmly unhook my bra and drop it to the ground. My nipples pearl up under her gaze, betraying me.

"Hi Jack." Her voice has a tease to it, like she's trying not to laugh. Suddenly I just need to be in the tub, not standing here putting on a show for her. I shuck off my basic underwear and almost stumble trying to get into the tub as quickly as I can.

She slides forward to make room for me to sit behind her and I sink into the water, my thighs sliding around her body like they've been there a million times.

Every nerve in my body is on fire. And then she leans back against me.

"You shouldn't be here," she says quietly, her voice a sigh against my body.

"I want to be," I whisper against her hair. She tips her head to the side, exposing her neck to me and it takes everything in me to stay still. She reaches for a bottle of body wash and squeezes a handful into a washcloth. As she lathers it up, I can feel something building—a sense that she wants to say more.

"What is it?" I ask, and she turns her head, glancing sideways to catch my eye for a second before turning back to focus on the soap. She slowly strokes the washcloth over her leg, the watery turning a sickly orange.

It should bother me.

It doesn't.

"I just feel compelled. I can't stop, Jack. And you'll want to stop me. I feel compelled to fix what men like him broke in me. And you feel compelled to stop me. It's a game that won't end well."

"I don't know if that's what I want anymore," I admit. "I want to protect you."

"Oh Jack," she murmurs, her voice tinged with sadness. "You're too good to protect someone like me."

"I don't feel *good*. I admit what you're doing." The realization crashes into me like a blow to the chest. I take in a jagged breath. "I feel guilty, but it's true."

Something shatters between us. She rolls over in the

water, her hand sliding up to cup my jaw. I clutch the sides of the tub, when every instinct screams to run my hands down her curves. But she's vulnerable—split wide open right now. I can't.

Her lips hover near mine, her breasts teasing against mine as she slides her body closer. I slip down in the water a little as our bodies merge together. She looks up at me, her lashes fluttering close to my face.

Her tongue darts out over her bottom lip before she leans forward, her lips just barely grazing against mine. She says my name against my mouth, a sigh as she guides my hand down her body.

My resolve cracks as my hand glides over her breast and down her rib cage. I pause at her waist, my fingers caressing her hip. She urges my hand down and gasps when my fingers glide between her legs.

I've forgotten who I am or what I stand for. The only thing I know is that Bunny is all I want and all I need right at this moment.

CHAPTER ELEVEN

I WAKE up knowing my entire world has just shifted. I don't know exactly what it holds, but I know there is no going backward.

The smell of coffee entices me to open my eyes and roll over. The other side of the bed is empty, but the pillow is still depressed where Bunny's head lay last night. Sliding out from under the sheets, I find a t-shirt and pair of shorts Bunny has left on a chair next to the bed. Gratefully, I slip into them and follow the scent out into the kitchen.

Bunny is sitting at the kitchen table, hands wrapped around a mug of steaming coffee. She looks smaller this morning, curled into herself. She's wired—coiled like a spring.

She's left a mug for me next to the coffee pot, so I pour myself a cup and add a splash of the creamer she has out, before joining her at the table.

I sit down across from her, and she glances up, her face unreadable.

"Relax," I say, my voice raspy. She forces a smile, stirs her coffee and then meets my eye again.

"They're hunting me." It's barely a whisper.

"Who is?" I ask, easily slipping back into my detective role.

"Local guys. There's a pretty big trafficking organization. Works out of some of the old abandoned warehouses." She looks down at her hands and studies her fingernails, refusing to meet my eye. She's like a caged animal, feeling trapped. I know this is what will make her careless.

"Bunny. What are you thinking? What did you do?"

"It's not what I did. It's what I'm going to do."

And there it is—the escalation I've known was building. She's spiraling again. Acting first, thinking never.

"Bunny," I repeat. She looks up, conviction written across her face.

She leans forward, her voice low. "There's someone above them. A real sadist. The others answer to him, and he's the one who gave the order to put me in the ground." Her voice trembles, but her eyes remain steady on me. "So I'm going to end him first."

Something cold crawls up my spine. "You're talking about killing the boss of the whole ring."

"I'm talking about surviving," she snaps. Then she looks away, jaw tight, before her face softens. "Jack... he won't stop. Not while I'm alive."

"Then we make him stop the right way. The legal way."

She laughs—brittle. Raw. "There's no legal way with men like him. You know that better than anyone."

"Bunny, listen to me." I reach across the table for her hand, but she pulls back like I burned her. I squash the feeling that evokes and press on. "This isn't self-defense. This is suicide."

She shakes her head, her curls swishing against her shoulders. "No. This ends with him or with me."

The words land like a punch. She means them. Every syllable is like a door slamming shut.

I look at her—the girl who turned her trauma into a weapon, who cleans up the night because no one ever cleaned it up for her. She's hunted by the traffickers, hunted by the law, and somehow still stalking the dark like she owes it something. And now she's cornered, ready to bare her teeth and die.

I realize I can't let her kill him.

And I can't let him kill her.

There's a third outcome—I just don't know what the hell it is yet. But I know one thing; whatever happens next, I'm already in it with her.

I push my coffee aside, lean in, and say, "Then we're going to find another way. Because I'm not losing you to him. And I'm damn sure not losing you to yourself."

Bunny doesn't reply. She just watches me, eyes shining like a warning or a promise. Maybe both.

Outside, a truck backfires and she flinches again.

Yeah—she's being hunted.

But now so am I.

CHAPTER TWELVE

I HEAD BACK to my motel, needing a change of clothes. A moment to breathe without her intoxicating presence.

But I spend the day pacing my small room. It's hard to think about anything but her.

When evening comes, I head out again and find myself standing next to her building, hidden by the eaves of the building next door. I'm feeling that now-familiar draw to just be here now. I don't know why, but I know I need to be.

It's not long before I see her slipping out of the door, looking around quickly as her pace picks up.

I don't tail Bunny so much as shadow her—close enough to stop her, far enough she won't sense the drag in her wake. She walks fast, hood up, shoulders squared like she's bracing for a punch that's overdue. The streetlights smear across the wet pavement, turning her into a long, wavering silhouette that wavers every time she stumbles on uneven sidewalk.

She never once checks behind her. That's how I know

she's in trouble. She cuts through a strip of shuttered galleries, then across a parking lot that smells like rain and rust. She heads toward the abandoned luxury condos near the water—once meant to be high-end, now just hollow towers slowly sinking into the fog. A perfect hideaway for people who don't want their work seen. I slip into the shadows as she ducks between two service vans and through a half-open maintenance gate. When I reach it, she's already partway up a scaffolding tower lining the side of the building.

No hesitation. No fear. Just a quiet, furious momentum.

I climb after her, slower, testing each rung. The metal is slick with mist, and every groan of the structure feels like an accusation. When I reach the fourth-floor balcony, Bunny's already climbed higher, a quick flash of motion disappearing through a cut glass pane someone prepared ahead of time—clean, precise, and deliberate.

She planned this. Alone. I step into the building.

Inside, the place feels like an unfinished skeleton. Bare concrete, exposed wiring, missing doors. The air carries dust and something else—an unclean stillness. My footsteps echo faintly, but her steps are silent, distant, almost imagined.

I track the faint shift of air in the stairwell. She's already above me. A few floors up, I glimpse her silhouette —hood gone, replaced by the kitten head mask.

Something about the way she climbs now is off.

Too fast. Too tense.

The kind of speed that doesn't come from confidence, but from panic.

On the fifteenth floor landing, she stops in front of a reinforced door with a single light glowing weakly overhead. A pale buzz fills the hallway. She presses her ear to the door, posture taut as wire.

I hear laughter inside—boastful, careless, the kind of sound men use when they think they own the dark.

Bunny breathes in once.

Then slips her prybar into the seam. The door yields with the smallest sigh. She disappears through the crack.

I'm seconds behind her, knowing how stupid this is. Without my weapon.

The room beyond is large—open floor plan, half-finished walls, construction dust on everything. Long tables hold phones, ledgers, unidentifiable equipment. Mattresses sit in corners. The space has the unmistakable feel of a place used often, cleaned rarely, and never for anything good. I slip into the shadow of a pile of old equipment. Remaining out of sight.

There are three men inside with her. And they don't notice her until she wants them to. Bunny moves with a strange, calm precision. Each step is measured, each strike efficient. She handles the first man before he even realizes she's entered the room—a blade across the throat. Clean and calculated. The second comes at her, and she swings at him with the prybar with practiced momentum, sending him stumbling back.

It's almost elegant—something like a dance, but with stakes that make breathing feel optional.

I've never seen her fight before. Tonight, she isn't pulling punches.

The third man reaches under the table, and I see his hand closing around something metal. I'm about to alert Bunny that he has a gun, but she's already noticed.

Before he can lift the weapon, Bunny intercepts him.

The struggle is quick but messy—desperate, almost frantic. Their fight knocks over a chair, a stack of files scattering across the floor.

"Bunny!" I shout, almost involuntarily, but she's locked in.

Too locked in.

While she's occupied, I spot movement near the far wall.

Another man steps out—the one she was warned about. The one running operations in this building. Older. Calm. Watchful. His confidence is a warning in itself.

He takes in the scene with a measured sweep of his eyes, then reaches subtly toward his ankle. I know that gesture too well. A hidden weapon.

"Bunny!" I call out again, louder.

She turns, just enough to see him advancing. One final kick and the man she was grappling with slumps to the floor.

I move. Instinct. Training. Something in between.

I intercept him before he reaches her, knocking his arm away. He's strong, but I've dealt with men like him. The fight between us is fast, a flurry of grappling and leverage. He tries to regain control; I refuse to give it.

Bunny recovers and steps in. Together, without speaking, we tip the balance—my force and her agility converging on him before he can regain footing.

The struggle that follows is chaotic, desperate, and nothing like the clean takedown she attempted earlier. He fights with the ferocity of someone who believes he cannot lose. Bunny fights with the ferocity of someone who believes she has to win.

Between the three of us, momentum shifts rapidly—shoves, blocks, hands grasping for advantage. The man tries for his hidden weapon again, but Bunny reacts faster this time. She cuts off his attempt and forces him away from me, driving him back across the room. The weapon skitters across the floor toward me. I lean down and pick it up without thinking.

For a moment, it looks like she'll retreat after disabling him. For that brief moment, I think I've reached her in time.

But her posture changes—shoulders squared, head lowered, breath sharp.

She sees not just a threat. She sees the man who put a price on her life. She sees every man who ever hurt her.

The room seems to compress, narrowing down to only Bunny and her target. She advances. He refuses to step back. Their final clash is decisive, swift, fueled by every injury she's carried and every fear she refuses to show.

When it's over, the man drops. Bunny stands over him, chest heaving.

Silence fills the room, thick and absolute.

Her mask is tilted slightly, the stitched kitten smile incompatible with the way she's shaking—an aftershock of adrenaline, fury, and something close to grief.

I realize my hands are on his weapon. My prints. My involvement. My choice.

Bunny turns toward me slowly, as if only now noticing I'm here. Her voice is barely audible when she says, "Jack..."

It isn't triumph. It isn't fear of him. It's fear of what we've crossed together. The man's body lies still between us.

And the darkness in this room settles like dust on our clothes, sealing itself into the seams.

There's no clean exit now. Not for her. Not for me.

We're tied to this moment—twisted together in a way neither of us planned.

And whatever comes next… we'll have to face it side by side.

CHAPTER THIRTEEN

A FLURRY of sound coming from the hallway alerts us that we soon won't be alone. Bunny jumps into action, jerking her head toward a window. She opens it to the fire escape landing and slips out.

I follow. Sliding the window closed behind me, I look up where she's already rapidly climbing. There's no time to think about the fact that I'm following a criminal, trusting her to get us to safety.

I climb.

When we finally reach the roof, we climb over. I turn and check the fire escape—no one is on it. So they didn't think to look there for us. An exhale of relief.

Suddenly the air is cold and clean again. I suck it in like I've just surfaced from drowning. My legs are shaking from the climb, the adrenaline. From everything that just transgressed.

From chasing Bunny.

Bunny is already ahead of me, boots thudding on the gravel as she crosses the rooftop. Her silhouette cuts sharply against the dying orange of the city lights—tall, decisive, built for motion. I drag myself after her, my lungs burning.

We leap the small gap between buildings. She makes it gracefully; I barely catch the far ledge with my fingertips. Gravel skids under my palms. For a second I'm falling. I kick at the building, trying to get a toe grip on something.

Then her hand clamps around my wrist.

Bunny hauls me up with a grunt, and when I'm upright again our faces are too close—her breath mixing with mine, the air crackling with something sharp. Something dangerous.

"Don't look at me like that," I whisper, even though I don't know what *that* is—fear? Anger? Hunger?

She doesn't let go of my wrist. Her fingers dig in. "If I hadn't grabbed you—"

"But you did," I shoot back. "So don't make it something else. I'm okay. We're okay."

Her jaw flexes. She releases me at last, stepping back like the space between us is the only thing keeping the rooftop from tilting.

Below, sirens slice through the night. The city pulses—alive, ravenous, hunting. I can feel it inside me too. It doesn't make sense. I should be hunting Bunny. But eliminating someone truly dangerous to society—to children and women… it made me zing with life. I feel more alive than I ever have before.

That's the moment I understand. This is more than just healing trauma for Bunny. This is giving her power. This euphoric high is what she's been feeling—what's been building for her.

"We can't keep doing this," Bunny says. She's not looking at me now; she's scanning the horizon, the alleyways, the sky. Anywhere but my eyes. "Running. Fighting. Dragging you deeper."

It's as though she read my mind.

A bitter laugh escapes me. "Dragging? You think I'm being dragged?"

"Jack." My name sounds like a warning in her mouth. "Listen to me." She finally faces me, and there's something raw in her expression—an unmasked worry she usually doesn't let anyone see. "If you walk away now, you can still be saved. This isn't you."

Saved. That word hits me like a wrecking ball.

She believes it. She truly does. That I'm still the woman I was before all of this, before her, before the spiraling choices that led us to a rooftop with blood drying on our clothes and sirens wailing our names.

I step closer. The wind pushes my hair across my face. "Maybe I don't want to be."

Her breath catches. The first crack in her armor tonight.

"Jack…" she murmurs. A warning, or a plea—I can't tell.

But I feel the truth vibrating between us, a taut wire stretched tight. We're too close to stop, too changed to go back, too dangerous to keep pretending this is survivable.

Below us, the city howls. It goes on, oblivious to the way my life just changed forever.

I meet her gaze, steady. "You didn't drag me. I'm here because I chose to be. Maybe I didn't know that at first. I was just chasing blindly. But deep down—I knew."

Bunny shakes her head once, sharply, like she's trying to dislodge the words before they take root. But they do. I can see it. I can feel it.

For the first time tonight, she looks afraid. Not of the

men hunting her. Not of the bodies she's left behind. But of us. Of what we are becoming. Together.

"Come on," she says at last, voice low. "We need to move."

She turns, but I stay still for one more heartbeat, letting the wind cool the fire under my skin.

Saved. It reverberates. Maybe I don't want to be.

I follow her across the rooftop, and the night swallows us whole.

By the time I reach my motel, my pulse has finally dropped below "flight-or-fight-or-die," but my hands still tremble as I slip the key into the lock. The door clicks open.

Inside, the room is exactly as I left it, which somehow feels worse than if someone had tossed it. My evidence file glows from the desk. Photos, notes, scattered across the top. Connections that once made sense to me. Next to it, my laptop blinks with paused footage. Bunny's face freezes mid-sentence, eyes shadowed, jaw tight.

I step in and shut the door behind me. The quiet hits like a blow.

All the evidence I've collected over the last few months —interviews with witnesses, shaky cell video from crime scenes, police radio logs I shouldn't have access to, and then… everything about her.

If I turned this in, it would end everything.

Every chase. Every night with adrenaline in my teeth. Every stolen breath on a rooftop.

Every piece of Bunny I've let myself keep.

I walk to the desk and touch the corner of a photo of her.

I could drag this whole bloody chapter into the daylight. Call my captain. Hand over the proof. Pretend I never crossed the line with her. Or.

Or… my other hand slips unconsciously toward the lighter in my pocket.

I could destroy it all. Erase her. Save myself.

My stomach twists because both options feel equally impossible. Just as I reach for the laptop, my phone vibrates.

CAPTAIN RUIZ flashes across the screen.

I swallow hard and answer. "Jack."

"Where are you?" he asks, no preamble, voice gravel-sharp. "You sound out of breath."

"I—I went for a run," I say, which is technically true if you ignore the gunfire. "Long day."

"Long night," he corrects. "We've had reports. Whispers of some kind of… female vigilante. Maybe you were right."

Every muscle in my body goes rigid.

He continues, "Witnesses say she's fast, violent, untrained but effective. Doesn't match any of our usual players." A pause. "You hear anything?"

I'm staring right at Bunny's frozen face on my laptop screen. Her earlier words echo. *If you walk away now, you can still be saved.*

My throat closes. "No," I say, too fast. The lie stumbles out, clumsy. "Nothing like that. Probably just the usual rumor mill."

Another pause—longer, heavier.

"Jack," Ruiz says slowly, "you're a terrible liar."

My fingers tighten on the phone.

"And I get the sense," he adds, voice dropping, "that you've stepped into something you don't know how to get out of."

I force a laugh. It sounds brittle. "I think I just need sleep, Captain. Just been helping out with my aunt. Family is… tough." The lie falls between us. For him to accept or call me out.

"Yeah." He doesn't believe me. I can hear it. "We'll talk soon. Are you coming back Monday?"

"I… I need some more time," I choke out.

"Wednesday then," he snaps. He hangs up before I can reply.

The silence that follows is deafening. The lighter in my pocket suddenly feels like a live wire.

Turn it in.

Burn it all.

Save myself.

Be lost forever.

Maybe I'd be lost forever either way.

I look back at Bunny's frozen expression—somewhere between defiance and regret. "What have you done to me?" I whisper to the room.

But the real question, I know, though…

Is… what have *I* done to myself?

CHAPTER FOURTEEN

THE BELL over the coffee shop door jingles as I step inside, and for a moment the warmth hits me so hard I almost mistake it for safety. The place is half-empty. A few students hunched over laptops, a barista cursing over one of the coffee machines, and the bitter scent of espresso thick in the air.

Bunny sits in the corner booth, hood up, hands wrapped around a mug she's not drinking from. She looks out of place here—too sharp, too coiled, a knife pretending to be a spoon in the silverware drawer.

She spots me instantly. Of course she does. She has more cop instincts than most of the colleagues I've worked with over the years.

I slide into the seat across from her. She doesn't smile.

"We shouldn't do this in public," she mutters.

"Then why'd you pick here?" I raise an eyebrow.

She looks down at her coffee, shrugging. "Neutral ground."

Neutral. Yeah okay. As if such a thing even exists between us anymore.

Before I can speak, she says, "I'm leaving." Her voice is flat but her knuckles are white around the mug. "I need to vanish for a while. Maybe longer." She hesitates, then adds quietly, "I won't let you burn your life down for me."

I knew it was coming. But it still hits me like a punch to the gut. I lean forward, keeping my voice low. "You don't get to decide that."

Her head snaps up. We lock gazes. "I'm trying to keep you safe. Do the right thing."

"By running away? Shutting me out? Deciding for me? Don't," I snap.

She flinches. Subtly, but I see it.

The espresso machine gurgles loudly, breaking the spell for a moment.

"Jack…" She exhales. "You don't understand what happens to people who get close to me."

I reach across the table and lightly touch her wrist. She doesn't pull away, but she goes still—like contact is a trap she walked willingly into.

"Then explain it," I whisper.

Her voice drops to a rasp. "I'm not afraid of prison. Or running. Or whatever comes next." Her eyes lift to mine, finally, and the vulnerability there nearly undoes me. "But you—losing you—Jack, that's the one thing I don't know how to survive."

For a heartbeat, the world goes silent. Even the coffee shop noise blurs into nothing.

The truth spreads around us like a gaping wound.

Duty tugs at me. My badge, my promises, everything I'm supposed to be, what I'm supposed to stand for. Desire pulls the other direction—toward her, toward the danger, toward the version of myself I'm terrified to admit I want.

Bunny isn't any better off. I can see the war in her eyes.

Freedom on one side, connection on the other. One means safety. The other means me.

"This can't end well," she says softly.

"I know." I don't break eye contact.

"But you're still here."

"And so are you." I smile. The corner of her mouth lifts just slightly. Not quite a smile.

Then she lets out a strangled kind of laugh. "Fuck, we're a mess." She shakes her curls.

But we don't leave. We sit there—two disasters pretending they're just people having coffee—dangerously close to choosing each other.

And dangerously close to losing everything else.

CHAPTER FIFTEEN

THE ALLEY behind the abandoned warehouse is quiet except for the low spit and crackle of the fire. A rusted metal barrel glows orange from the flames licking out of its top, the smell of burning paper curling into the night air.

My fingers hover over the folder one last time—photos, transcripts, clips of Bunny's voice, evidence that could bury her ten times over.

My entire career.

Her whole life.

I know she's watching from a few feet behind me. Arms crossed, waiting. Wanting me to choose her. Wanting me to walk away. Both at the same time. Feeling as conflicted as I do right now.

My heart pounds in my ears, drowning out the world. I drop the folder in and the flames hiss, welcoming the new fuel. The pages curl in the flames, pieces of ash breaking off and floating in the air around us.

Bunny makes a sound behind me, but I don't turn around. Not just yet.

"This at least buys you time," I say. It's not a decision. It's not a promise. It was a folder I wasn't supposed to have anyway. A hunt I wasn't supposed to be on.

The silence stretches on as the pages burn down to bits of nothing. She shifts behind me, her boots crunching on the ground.

She stops behind me, our shadows melting together, like the fire has decided we are now one. "Then stay with me," she murmurs. "Run with me."

The invitation is like a sharp blade plunged between my shoulder blades. I stare at her.

My mind spirals—duty clawing up my spine, justice whispering that I've lost my way, desire pulling me forward, danger humming like a second heartbeat.

Choosing Bunny means I leave everything I know, everything I once believed myself to be.

If I don't… I lose her. For good.

The fire cracks loudly, sending sparks into the air like frantic stars trying to escape. My mind swirls.

Captain Ruiz's suspicion.

My badge.

My oath.

Bunny's confession.

Bunny's fear.

My own.

The barrel spits out one last flame. Bright, high, and hungry. The last page curls inward and vanishes.

And in that suspended moment—caught between ruin and salvation, between the woman I am and the one I'm becoming—anything could still happen.

The choice hangs there, untouched, burning quietly between us.

Unmade.

CHAPTER SIXTEEN

THE ASHES BURN down to a dim glow, a barrel of red-rimmed embers breathing out the last of my old life. The alley is cold around us, the night thick with damp and danger. Bunny stands inches away.

She reaches out her hand, waiting.

Waiting for me to become something I'm not sure I recognize anymore.

I study her fingers—the small nicks, the faded scars at her wrist. Proof of the violence she's survived. Proof of what she's capable of. Proof of everything I should run from.

The city hums around us, a heartbeat all its own. The truth is simple, impossible, and heavier than any badge I've ever worn.

I'm done pretending I don't want what I want.

Even if I can't name it.

Even if it ruins me.

I take a breath that tastes like ash and cold air.

"For now..." I say, letting the words settle between us

like a weapon laid gently on a table, "I'll walk with you. But don't mistake that for surrender."

A beat of silence.

Then her smile—soft, crooked, dangerously hopeful blooms. It's the kind of smile that could unravel someone if they weren't already frayed.

"Wouldn't dream of it," Bunny murmurs.

I don't take her hand.

She doesn't force it.

Instead we fall into step, side by side, our shadows stretching together across the wet pavement as we slip out of the alley and into the din of the city.

No promises. No vows.

Just the sharp, electric knowledge that everything could still break—us, the law, the world we're choosing to walk through.

The future rises in front of us like a dark road with no map.

She pulls her hood up.

I bury my hands deep in my pockets.

And together, without ceremony or certainty, we disappear into the city's waiting glow—two silhouettes moving toward whatever tomorrow is brave or foolish enough to bring.

Unresolved. Unforgiven. Unfinished.

But walking forward, all the same.

www.ingramcontent.com/pod-product-compliance
Lightning Source LLC
LaVergne TN
LVHW051007080826
845145LV00009B/2497